TOO LATE

Also by Stephen Dixon
No Relief
Work

Stephen Dixon

NEW YORK
HAGERSTOWN
SAN FRANCISCO
LONDON

TOO LATE

Harper & Row, Publishers

1817

TOO LATE. Copyright © 1978 by Stephen Dixon. All rights reserved. Printed in the United States of America. No part of this book may be used or reproduced in any manner whatsoever without written permission except in the case of brief quotations embodied in critical articles and reviews. For information address Harper & Row, Publishers, Inc., 10 East 53rd Street, New York, N.Y. 10022. Published simultaneously in Canada by Fitzhenry & Whiteside Limited, Toronto.

FIRST EDITION

Designed by Sidney Feinberg

LIBRARY OF CONGRESS CATALOG CARD NUMBER: 77-6887
ISBN: 0-06-010053-2

*To the memory of Carole Madelaine Dixon
and James Robert Dixon*

TOO LATE

She says "This movie's much too violent for me, I've got to leave."

"Wait up, I'll go with you."

"No, stay. You wanted to see it more than I."

"But I don't like you going home alone."

"It's all right. Plenty of people out. I'll be safe."

"You can't wait in the lobby till it's through?"

"Will you hush it up down there please?" someone says.

"Wait in the lobby for me," I whisper.

"I don't want to. I've nothing to read. They've no seats there. Look, why do you think I'm so helpless? I can take care of myself."

"Okay, if you don't mind."

"I don't. See you." I stand so she can get by me.

"Sit down, sit down," someone behind us says.

"I have to get out," she says.

"Then get out but stop standing. You're blocking my view."

"What do you want her to do, crawl out on her knees?" I say.

"Yes." Someone else hoots back. Few people laugh. She grabs my hand and says "Don't bother with them, let it ride," and passes me. I want to kiss her hand but the man next to me says "Now you're in my way, miss," so I let her let go of my hand and I sit. She leaves. I watch the movie. It is too violent. During the worst scenes—man getting riddled with bullets and what looks like real blood dribbling out of real holes, woman strangled with wire and her face puffing up to almost twice its size—I have to cover my eyes with my hand. Couple times during those scenes I look around. No one has his eyes covered that I can see. Just about everyone's staring at the screen. In the end the killer flies off in a stolen helicopter and a lot of the audience applaud him. Maybe the actor deserved some applause but not this man. He was a butcher. All his victims were innocent. The movie wasn't worth sitting through. It was the last show and I leave with everyone else.

There are 3 fairly dark sidestreets I have to walk on to get home. I've a strange feeling someone's going to run up on me or jump at me from behind a parked car or out of one of the building cellars along the way and I walk faster. I hope the streets weren't as empty when Donna walked home. I think what would I do if she didn't get home all right and the thought scares me so much I put it out of my head. That movie was supposed to be a present-day account of crime in this city but to me the violence was greatly exaggerated. Every other time a woman rides the subway at night she doesn't get molested or mugged. A man can walk through most parks during the day without getting stabbed or robbed. The movie made this city seem like an armed camp. Teenagers do have pistols and shotguns in some parts of the city but don't roam around midtown with them threatening shopowners and pedestrians, nor do I think our policemen are afraid of these boys as much as the movie wanted me to believe.

Thinking about the movie makes me afraid for my own safety and I start to run home. I should have told Donna to take a cab, maybe taken one myself. Now I only want to know she's safe, to be in bed with her and have her head on my shoulder as she likes to do before she turns over and falls asleep. To tell her I was worried about her when I went home and that I love her very much, even though she probably won't say the same to me.

She'll say something like "That's nice to hear, you're my dearie too" and maybe kiss me or let me kiss her goodnight. Then if I try and get her to speak she'll get angry at me and maybe get up with her pillow to sleep in the other room.

She isn't home. I have a beer, turn the tv on and off, I'm to worried to watch it and I just wait. I wait 2 hours, 3. I try and read, try and sleep. I think something could be wrong but I don't want to call anyone yet. If she was staying out late or away for the night at someone's place she would've called. She's done it before. Couple weeks ago she called at 3 in the morning and said "I won't be coming home tonight." "You mean tonight after today?" and she said "Tonight." "Why not?" "I'm staying out." "Where?" "Friend's house." "Who?" "Someone." "A man friend?" "Yes." "So why'd you call then?" "I didn't want you to be worried." "I'm not worried." "Good." "I'm mad as hell at you for waking me past 3 to tell me this because now I won't be able to sleep thinking of you 2 screwing for an hour if you haven't already screwed for an hour and also in the morning screwing too" and hung up.

So maybe she hasn't called because she knows I'll snap at her if she does. But that night when she stayed with a man she was having dinner with him beforehand so I knew there was a chance she might stay over his place. "There's always some chance," she said once when she was leaving to meet a man for a movie or dinner or drinks, "since I never know exactly where it's going to lead." But tonight she didn't say anything to make me think she was meeting a man. She said she'll see me home. But maybe this man from a couple weeks ago or another one phoned after she got home and she met him and one thing led to another and she's now at a dance club or his place or something like that. I hope so.

I fall asleep and wake up. Stomach aches from all the beer I drank to put me to sleep and I take an antacid and wait for her. She doesn't come home or call. 5 o'clock, 6. I doze and wake. 10 o'clock, noon. I call her agency. "No," the receptionist says, "she's not scheduled to model today." I take a walk hoping she'll be home when I get back and to think about where she might be and why she might not have come home or called me. I walk to the pier, sit at the tip of it, watch pleasure crafts and cruise ships pass and listen to someone's radio from several feet away. Newscaster's speaking about a priest who was murdered in my neighborhood last night. I know the church. Just yesterday I saw people on my block soliciting donations to get the steeple clock repaired. "The 3 killers left the parish in a disarray and got away with only a handful of change." A bus driver was also knifed last night but in another borough when his assailant refused to believe he didn't have the key to the safe connected to the coinbox. "4 streetwalkers were gunned down this morning—"

"Will you please lower your radio," I say to the man holding it, "or play it somewhere not so close?"

"Why?"

"No reason. If I said 'It annoys me, it's too loud, it's an assault on my privacy, that I came here for some quiet and to think about important things to me and enjoy the sun and view'? I know. 'Tough.'"

"That's right, tough."

I move to the other side of the pier almost out of radio range. I watch a tanker coming in aided by 2 tugs. An argument begins near me. 2 men, one in soft black leather, other in a brief bathingsuit. Up until a minute ago they seemed to be good friends. Held hands, kissed each other's lips, recited poetry while the leather man sat on the other man's knees and played with his shaved skull. Then the bathingsuit man said "I don't care if sexual jealousy does sound antediluvian to you, I want a sworn oath you'll never see him again." The leather man says "You should know by now I never swear and that I do what the goddamn crap I please."

"Don't you speak to me like that."

"Order me around some more and I'll speak to you any crappy assed way I want and worse."

The bathingsuit man spits at him. Leather man wipes the saliva off his jacket and rubs it in the other man's face. Bathingsuit man pushes him off and stands and beats him on the chest with the poetry book they were alternately reading. Leather man lifts him by his armpits, throws him to the ground and squeezes his fists into the man's temples. Bathingsuit man opens his mouth but can't scream. Several of us surround the 2 men and say things like "Do you want him off you, stop hurting him, let him go, get your knuckles out of his head, he's turning blue," but do nothing to pull the leather man away.

"Stay out of it," the leather man says. "It's a family quarrel."

"No we won't stay out of it," I say.

"Step into it then, baby, and risk getting your own head crushed."

"Someone call the police," I say.

"We haven't time," a woman says. "He's killing him."

"Oh screw you all and this little turd ball" and he slaps the bathingsuit man's face, gets up, walks through the crowd, gets on a bicycle and rides away. The bathingsuit man lies on the ground crying. A woman kneels over him and pats his shoulder. I think of Donna and hope she's home. There's a phonebooth at the end of the pier. I put my sneakers on and run to it. The leather man's speaking with another man in a bikini near the end of the pier. He sees me and lets his bike drop and faces me with his fists raised and neck clenched as if I'm going to jump him but I run past.

Nobody answers our phone. I dial again, thinking I might've dialed the wrong number or the phone system hooked me into the wrong connection, but nobody answers. I cab home. "Donna," I yell opening the door, "Donna, you home?" She isn't. I call her best friend and she says "Yeah?"

"Joanne, it's me, look it—"

"Hey, how ya doing?"

"Fine thanks, but you've any idea where Donna might be or if she stayed the night with you or anyone you know?"

"No, anything wrong?"

"I'm not sure. We went to a movie last night. She left because it was too violent for her and said she was going straight home. She didn't say 'straight,' just that she'd see me home."

"That could mean different things. That she'd see you when you got home or after, later."

"Not almost a day later. To me it meant she'd be home when I got home and I'm sure she knew I'd head straight home after the movie. I in fact wanted to go home with her but she said she'd be safe and I should stay, and she isn't working today. So she either got home and left and hasn't come back since or not when I was there or never got home. I'm worried. There seems to be so much violence around us lately. In the movies, both on the screen and sort of in the seats behind us, rowdies threatening me or ready to when I asked them to quiet down. That happened last night too. Also a priest killed in a church nearby, a bus driver knifed, though in another borough. Even at the pier today. 2 homosexuals, one almost killing the other with this torturous forceps grip with his fists into the fellow's temples."

"What's their being homosexuals got to do with it?"

"Nothing I suppose, except one was dressed only in black leather from head to toes while the other was normally dressed for the sun in a bikini. And they seemed to like one another enough till their fight over sexual jealousy got out of hand. I'm not jealous, mind you, I mean of Donna, that's not what I'm implying. Except of course to the degree anyone who's close with someone is jealous if his or her partner is sleeping with or growing fond of someone else."

"Mark and I aren't jealous. He lets me see my lovers, I let him have his. He can even stay away for 2 weeks in a row for all I care and fall over his feet in love with her, so long as he assures me he'll be back in a month."

"That might be true, but usually—always—Donna's called when she was staying out. Last time it was with a man and I got mad at her more for waking me up so late with her call and making me think about her making love with this guy all night."

"People don't do it all night. Nobody does. Maybe only insects."

"I know. I'm exaggerating. And I don't think she stayed out with a man last night. But I would like his number, this fellow she saw 2 weeks ago if you have it. Or his name so I can get his number from the operator or phonebook. Maybe she stayed over his place again and is with him now. If that's so, I only want to know so I can stop worrying about her. Is that wrong you think?"

"I don't know if I should give it."

"Then you know who he is?"

"Donna told me how crazy you got that night and how scared she was to see you the next day. Some man ever acted like that to me, he and his bags would be out of my house in a minute."

"Believe me, if she isn't with him I don't know where else to look. I might even have to call the police."

"Don't. I'm sure it's nothing. There could be plenty of places she could be."

"Another man?"

"She is attractive and does get around. I've been with her. Guys flash on her in bakeries they ask for dates."

"First give me the one from 2 weeks ago."

"Sure you won't do anything rash to her if she does answer the phone?"

"Not on your life."

"You never know. All right. Louis Telegrin. Lives in the West 20s."

"Any others?"

"Listen, only other man I know for sure she's recently seen is someone I thought you knew about too. What was happening was at least obvious to me when you and they were at my party last month."

"Who?"

"Thomas. My younger brother. But I know she's not with him and wasn't because he slept here and is watching television now and except for Mark and the dogs we were alone."

I get Telegrin's number from the phonebook and call.

"Yo?"

"Hello, is Donna Akers around or anywhere you might know? This is a good friend."

"Why you think she be here? Not that I'm giving you her number, but you try her answering service or home?"

"I am at home. I live with her."

"Oh sorry, you're the one. No, she not here and where she would be I think you'd know more than me. But something real bad? Sounds it by your tone."

"Just that she didn't come home last night when there was no reason she shouldn't and neither today so I'm concerned. I'm sure it's nothing."

"I'm sure so too. Don't worry about her, she can take care of herself good, so she be back. But she get hold of me first, I tell her you called."

I wait. 6,7,8. I have a snack, take a nap, call Joanne. She says "Thomas and I phoned most of the spots she could be at and the latest anyone's seen or heard from her is early yesterday. Now you got us worried. You better call the police."

I call Donna's answering service. "Did Donna Akers call in today?"

"Let me see. Aaron, Acevedo, Akers, no."

"She does, tell her to call home? It's very important."

"Check," click.

I call the police. A detective asks me lots of questions, tells me to bring a picture of her in. I do. He holds it to the light and says "What was she last wearing at the movies?"

"Very simple. Gray espadrilles and faded blue denims—jacket, jeans and shirt. Her hair's short now, not like in the photo. Also her body's long and thin, flat breasts. She'd love to be built as big and wide as she looks here, but this was touched up by her modeling agency for a bra job she never got."

"Foot size? Just in case we get an impression somewhere that fits hers. And if you have a water glass with her fingerprints on it and how much you know about her teeth? They hers? Straight and so white like this picture and any other parts that might come off like a wig she could have had on that night or in her pocketbook or a hand even I mean where she could be more easily identified. I'm sure with a hand missing she couldn't've worked as a clothes model, but along those lines. A missing finger joint or toe. And any moles?"

"No."

"Then you can say you know her body pretty well then. No operation scars on her abdomen or disfiguring marks or pocks or blotches on her buttocks let's say or inner thighs or anywheres like there?"

"I don't remember a mark anywhere on her except for an embedded blackhead she's had in the small of her back for a number of years she said and which I wanted to pop once but she said it's been done and only a doctor can really take it out." I tell him I'll phone in her foot size from her shoes when I get home or if I can find an unwashed water glass she's used I'll come back tonight.

I wake around midnight and call the police. "No, no news. Your missing report's out to all the precincts. One other thing now that I got you. Her navel. You know if it's knotted in or out?"

"In, quite deep."

"No good then. A statetrooper found a woman who's as thin and young though not so tall as your Miss Akers but who's got surgical scars under both breasts and as for the navel it says here is a definite out."

Joanne calls at 2. "Didn't want to wake you but there is one other man I know Donna recently saw. I wouldn't tell you but for the reason she's missing like she is. Bartender at the Express. I met him with her a few nights ago, you were at a play. We had a beer at the bar and they started talking and before you know it they made a date for the next day and he's serving the rest of his customers, never another word or eye to us again except when he asks if we want refills. You want to check it out or just forget it?"

The Express is a couple blocks from me and I say to the bartender there "Excuse me but are you the bartender who knows Donna Akers?"

"Donna? Not Lorna? No? Donna, Donna, sounds familiar but don't know."

"Tall pretty woman, like a fashion model."

"Very big and slim with no tits or hips and those bony cheeks and short kinky black hair?"

"That's a permanent, yes. You've seen her today or maybe last night?"

"What are you, her big brother or lover who's come to cream me?"

"Just looking for her. We shared an apartment on a purely economic basis and she owes a few months' rent."

"No, she was only in once, last week, I don't know when and we balled the next day or so but that was it, never saw her again since. We both knew it was a one shot happening after it was over and didn't even waste our time getting each other's phone number."

"If you see her again could you tell her to call home where she lives?"

"Let me get this down. Bad memory. Donna. 2 n's. Big broad. Call landlord at home. Re rent. Right."

Home. Phone rings. "Louis here. Sorry but I call before and nobody in but she come back?"

"No."

"Maybe the police then, though you keep me out of it, what do you say?"

"They're already out searching but I didn't mention you."

"That's smart. Hey, I don't want to be croaching, know? I'm saying, you live with her so sure any other day but today you and me we don't speak so easy with each other. But she come back one of you 2 guys you call me just so I know she okay, okay?"

"We will. Thanks for your concern."

"Hey, she a good chick, I want to. But you don't have to call me so soon after she get home if she come later tonight. You 2 you want to talk. Me I want to sleep."

I call the police next morning. "Nothing. Something materializes, we'll contact you." I call my job and say I can't come in for a few days and my boss says "You don't come in you don't come in ever, understand? We don't need you to take a week off when we need you and you're not sick and craftsmen busting my door down for work and I'm tireder than you and me put together but do you see me taking off? No. But you sick?"

"No. A close friend."

"Well sick friend let him or her take care of themselves. You, you come in or don't again, that's your business and by noon."

"I want to be fair to you. My guess is I won't be in."

"I want to be fair too. I'll still give you till noon."

I go to the movie theater Donna and I went to that night. "You ask the same questions the police did for that show," the manager says, "and I'll tell you no different than what I told them. I don't remember a woman leaving the theater alone time you and they said she did and I'm always by the ticket booth except when I take a piss. And they said a very tall woman. Very skinny and pretty and I saw her picture and now you in front of me and don't remember seeing either of you here that night walking in or out. That might mean I was pissing when you both came in or when one of you went out but no chance I was pissing all 3 times when both you and she went in and out. You have your stubs?"

"I must've torn them to little shreds as I usually do when I get to my seat."

"That's what they all say when they want their money back because of a stomach attack 3 and a half hours after they walked in. But how do I know you're not saying you and her were here because of something you want to hide or she? No sir, I didn't see either of you in here and I've a head for faces like some do for names. I have to. At the cheap prices we charge we get some real duds who I can't let in if they paid 5 times as much."

"Maybe to prove it—no, I could've seen the same show someplace else. But there were a group of rowdies that night you might remember. Making all sorts of noises and smoking and drinking beer in the no smoking section and passing around lit joints and causing one couple near us to go back to the manager they said they were doing to get them thrown out."

"That happens every night or just about, what else is new? Why do you think I stick by the booth weeding the worst ones out? No, I never saw you before or your skinny girl and that's what I'm telling the cops next time they ask."

"Mind if I speak to your cashier?"

"You recognize her from that night?"

"No, well, I think so—it's her, isn't it?"

"That thief? Dollar for me, 2 for her—she lasted one week. I canned her last night. She didn't recognize your girlfriend either she told the police. Even if she had she wouldn't have told the truth, for less she has with the law the better for her."

The detective calls me. "A young woman's been picked up in the river, her body. Description fits a lot closer than yesterday's woman and she isn't too decomposed, 2 days at the most. Tall, short black hair, thin physique. No identifying marks or blackhead on her back, but someone said so long in the water could've popped that. No clothes on or silver chain round her waist you said she always wore and never took off, not even marks where the chain might've been. That's not unusual, could've rubbed off. And if some poor dumb sonofabitch hyena killed her before he dumped her, he would've taken the chain and tried selling it on the street for what he could get. That's why we rarely find those things like rings when we dredge. Could you come down? This affecting you too much, I could send a car to pick you up."

I go to the morgue. Attendant has to hold my arm as she leads me in. I'm shaking, saying "It can't be, has to be not."

"Just be calm, look only at the face and give yourself as much time as you like. You feel yourself fainting or throwing up, warn me."

She pulls the cloth away. Young woman, something like Donna. Big nose and fat cheeks though, not slim with high bones, but maybe the time in the water filled them up. Can't see her eyes but a card on the sheet says "blue" while Donna's were black. "Resembles my friend," I say being led out, "but far as I know I've never seen that woman before."

"I could tell right off. Otherwise I wouldn't have hustled you out so fast. Want a coffee? Like to rest? Though maybe it's best you go home."

Home. Joanne calls, Louis. She says "It looks bad," he "I hate to say it but I begin to give up hope." Her dad calls. "Hello, how are you, everything's dandy with me, can you get Donna please?"

"Not in."

"Have her call me. Tell her it's nothing to get excited about and that this time I won't lift the receiver unless she calls collect."

"Will do." I go to sleep, call the police next morning. "We already said. Anything new, we'll call you." Her dad calls.

"She didn't come home last night."

"Why not? Everything all right between you 2?"

"Sure, everything's fine."

"Then why didn't she come home? She away? Staying with a friend?"

"I don't know. I want to tell the truth. She didn't call."

"Why not? When she stays away for the night, doesn't she phone you?"

"We don't make it an issue. I've stayed out a few nights too without calling or telling her beforehand I wasn't coming home."

"She's been away a few nights?"

"No. Only 2, 3."

"3? Without phoning you? How could she? And you? Don't either of you think the other will be worried?"

"We just take for granted the other's okay and doing what the other wants to do and is able to handle his or herself while he or she's doing it, whatever it is."

"How can you? I know everyone young is supposed to be so cool and hung loose and hippily relaxed and all that, dig, man, give me 5? But neither of you are that young anymore and in your city you should be anxious if not alarmed and out of your mind if the other stays away without saying he or she is planning to. And after 3 nights you should be on your knees trying to revive your dead god so you can beseech him."

"Take it easy, Gabe. I know it'll be all right."

"How do you know? Why you so cocksure? This is my one and only daughter, our single child from siblingless parents of a matro-patroclinal line of more than 300 years here. I've no wife left, no relatives, nobody I can authentically call my friend anymore. Donna's my sole soulmate, psychosexuality defenestrated. You don't ease me one iota with your assurances. I'm calling back tonight at 7. Be there. Donna contacts you or gets home before then have her call me immediately. You hear from her before but for some reason she can't make another call, you call me."

"Right." I call the police. Sleep. Eat. Drink. Joanne calls. Gabe. "She hasn't called or come home."

"Then phone the police."

"I don't want to make a big deal out of it."

"Then I'm phoning them."

"Don't."

"Why not goddamn you you heartless indifferent slob?"

"Because I've called them."

"Then you are worried. What's wrong?"

"We've never once stayed out a single night without telling

the other beforehand or at least called. And I've never stayed out since we began living together while Donna has with me, several times, a few."

"Then you should have quit her if she did that with another man which I'm assuming from what you said that she did and you never did it with her and maybe then she wouldn't be missing now for 3 nights."

"I don't see how that makes any sense."

"I'm coming right down. If I run now I can make the next bus. If I miss it I'll be on the following one. They leave every hour till 10. Check the schedules so you can meet me. They each take 90 minutes nonstop. If I don't see you I'll phone from the terminal. Be there, one place or the other."

Soon after speaking to him the downstairs buzzer rings. I press the intercom talk button and say "Donna?"

"Police. She get hold of you since the last time we spoke?"

"No. I thought she might've forgotten her keys and was ringing to be let in."

"Why?"

"You want to come up?"

"Yes we want to come up. But her keys. She leave them with you or anywheres you know?"

"If you don't mind I don't want to speak through this thing. I'll tell you when you get upstairs." I ring them in, open the door while they're climbing the last flight. "I didn't mean to be rude to you just now but I thought it was Donna downstairs only because I just hoped it was her and that she'd forgotten her keys or couldn't get to them, that's all."

"She left her keys here?"

"I haven't seen them."

"Did you see her take them?"

"I don't know, I don't remember."

"If she didn't, maybe that's why she first stayed out. Because she couldn't get in. What might have happened to her after that is another matter. But that's pure spec. Not a word of fact to it."

"Let me think. No, I don't remember seeing her leave or take her keys. Let me tell you something though. Whenever we went out together we always took a set of keys apiece, unless she forgot to, I never did. Reason is we once had an argument on the subway and she wanted to get off at the next stop and take the subway home. She asked me for my keys because she didn't bring hers with her since she felt why should she if I had mine and we were going to the same place together that night. It was a concert. I wouldn't give her mine though. I didn't want her to go home without me and I didn't want to go home yet or go to the concert alone. We already had tickets. I also thought the concert would be much more enjoyable if I went with her. So we stayed on the subway, she reluctantly, but constantly badgering me for my keys till I gave them to her and went to the concert alone and she went home. Much later she had to let me in. I'd stopped off for a beer on the way home. She was already asleep. For that reason also, that I woke her hours after she went to sleep, even if it was because I didn't have my keys to get in since she'd taken them, she vowed that whenever she left the house with me she'd always take her own keys. That's why I think that when we went to the movies she took her keys."

"How long ago was that?"

"The subway argument? Months."

"You've had fights like that since?"

"Sure we've had fights. We didn't always get along. Who does? Maybe a few. But I'd say 25 percent of our waking time together we didn't get along, or maybe 20 percent. But a large enough percent to make us unsure of ourselves together a lot of the times or at least to make our relationship seem precarious, vulnerable, one of those, definitely not certain. A word—uncertain—you know, though most times together we felt medium good to great. 10 percent would be closer to when it wasn't that good or plain bad. Actually about 5 percent was plain bad, at least 5, for it went on for hours, the hate and hostility, sometimes for a day and 2 nights, so I'd settle on 15 percent when it was very bad or just not good."

"I wonder what it is with my own wife."

"With my wife," another detective says, "the percentages are just the reverse."

"What, 10 to 20 percent of your sleeping time you get along? Look," to me, "we want to inspect your apartment. We don't suspect you. And it's not your subway arguments or about the keys. We came here with the intention of inspection. But we have to moderately suspect everyone and everything about her now that she's been gone for 4 nights."

"After tonight will be the fourth."

Looks in his notebook. "You're right."

3 of them check my sheets, laundry in our laundry bag, the laundry bag, dresser drawers, shoebag, closets, clothes, all the pockets and sleeves of our clothes, shoes and boots and slippers on the closet floors. They want to see my wallet. "That is if it's okay with you. You can say no."

"No, anything you want to see, see."

My wallet, pockets in my shirt and pants. Everything in my pants. Hanky, coins, comb, pen, keys. My hands, fingernails, hair. "We'd like a scraping from here, just a little snip of your hair from there. It won't show. You're curly and it can be combed back and covered like it was never cut. I'm straight so with me if he did it it might tell." Both dropped into see-through envelopes and taped and marked, nail scraping I can't see. "You don't have to but can we look over your whole body now? All the way? Undressed?"

"Can I undress in the bathroom?"

"Do it where you want, why even ask?"

"I thought maybe you didn't want me in there alone because whatever you're looking for you might think I might try and hide."

"What could you hide? Like if there was a recent knife slice or scratches you couldn't explain, you couldn't hide them behind the medicine chest or under a floor tile, right? For that's truthfully what we're looking for when we conduct a full body search. Nothing that you might have stuck up your ass. I'm telling you this every step of the way so you know we're not trying to pull anything over on you and everything's clear. We're just doing the normal. She's missing, you lived with her, so we also want to know about you. I personally feel you're not involved if there is anything wrong and that you care for her very very much."

"You could even be telling me this—"

"I'm not, I mean it I'm not. Maybe to some we work over our lines before because we have to but not to you."

"Even there—"

"What do you want me to say? Sure because we're here in such force you might feel we suspect you if just a little but we absolutely don't. He doesn't, he doesn't and I don't. Now please get undressed. That is, if you don't mind. You do, say so and we stop and won't be suspicious of you even one bit more than we were before which was nothing, zero percent. You have every right not to undress. To even not speak to us. You can even ask us to leave. You can have a lawyer here while we're here. Anyone here, your mother even may she rest in peace if that's where she is. You can refuse to breathe even. You name it. What?"

"I don't mind undressing. Not that this is helping, but I want to help all I can."

"It is helping. Quicker we get rid of you we can go on to other things about her and maybe find her which is what you want, true?"

"Of course. Excuse me." I undress in the bathroom, come out in a bathrobe, drop it, turn around as his finger directs me to. They inspect. "Now if you'll lie on your stomach on the floor? On your back? You've a brown lump here. You should check into it. Great." I get dressed. They inspect the bathrobe I left on the floor, the floor, under the rug. They roll up the rug and inspect the area the rug was on. "May we?" and I say "Whatever" and they look inside the table and desk drawers.

"You through with the rug?"

"Sure, roll it back."

I sweep up the rug area first.

Windows, sills, ledges, backyards with their flashlights, radio, television, medicine chest, pill bottles, "Anything you don't want us to look at, say."

"No, it's all okay."

Kitchen, cabinets, hatrack, her job portfolio. "Mind?"

"No."

Unzippers it. "This is a much better photo of her I think. Can we have it?"

"I'll get it back?"

"Everything we take or took of hers will be returned. You want the photo you gave us the other day, it's yours. Here, I'll give you an acquisition slip for each. At least I thought I had those on me. Doug, you have a take slip?"

"No gots."

"God are we the dumb cops. I'll just write down on something what I took and sign it. This envelope mean anything to you?"

"No."

"Then I'll use it. One, 'photo of face, waist up, of Miss Akers. Fur cap and jacket on, hair windblown, fur belt too. Taken for what looks like an ad for mink.'"

"Fake fur."

"Could have fooled me. Look at this, Doug. Anything ever look so real? Second photo's a full face one, longer hair, body touched up for possible bra jobs, right?"

Inside the fireplace, books, diaries on the bookshelf. "Whose are these?"

"Hers. She wrote in it about once a week. I've never read any of them. She never wanted me to though I knew they were there."

"Mind if we open them?"

"That I don't know."

"If she had them on the shelf in open view she must have known people would see and read them."

"I don't think she saw it that way."

"You're the boss. Though we could always get some kind of writ to read them. Tomorrow, day after. You want to help, why waste our time?"

"Because they're not mine. I know she'll hate anyone going through them."

"Then she should have stored them, no?"

"She trusted people. She knew I wouldn't touch them. And with her name and the word diary on them, she knew other people we knew who might browse through the shelves wouldn't too. But she'll just have to understand we're doing this only to help in some way."

"Sure she will. How couldn't she?" Opens it. Other detectives open 2 of the other diaries. "Hm. Last entry. It says here you had an awful fight she says here a few days ago."

"Not a fistfight. Verbal. We never got past the lips brawling. I've never once I don't think used my hands on her in the 3 years."

"Funny, because it also says same entry she was afraid you were going to bust her one like she says in her own words 'he poked me in the nose nearly a year ago almost knocking me out.'"

"Not out. I forgot. Her cheek. More of a slap. She forgets too you know. Look it up. I'm sure she wrote it down. And you can't come near to knocking someone out with just a slap. She wanted to move out. I didn't want her to nor had the rent money to stay here alone and called her all sorts of names. Whore, bastard. She said something back very bitchily and already like ready to burst I slapped her hard with my opened hand. That's the only time. Though for all I know now, maybe I forgot the other times too."

"Why'd you call her a whore?—Excuse me, but why, if you want to answer. I'm curious."

"I was only trying to remember why, not getting out of the question. She was sleeping with another man about twice or 3 times a month and I didn't want her to."

"Why?"

"Why? Why do you think?"

"I don't know, why?"

"Because I wanted her to only sleep with me, why else? I was jealous and didn't want to go along with the double standard she wanted me to and so I screamed the easiest and most accessible insult I guess. Whore, prostitute, whatever, I forget. Maybe the exact word's in her diary too. But I get stupid and very excitable sometimes like that."

"Makes sense. That situation, what man doesn't?"

"I know loads of men who'd love other men's wives to sleep with them," Doug says.

"Did I hear my ears right?" one questioning me says.

"You don't?"

"But you're so funny sometimes. You come into the conversation as if you heard everything when you didn't. We're not speaking about sleeping with other men's wives but one's own wife. These 2 weren't married, aren't, but it was the same thing to him, is, right?"

"Right," I say. "I've thought about sleeping with other women as most husbands do. Thought about it but didn't, in 3 years, while she did."

"She's slept with other women's husbands or just other women too? I'm sorry, but I'm mixed up, which?"

"Now you're kidding me as he was."

"Believe me, Doug wasn't kidding and neither am I. Does she switch?"

"No, not that I know for sure. But I'm almost sure not. I mean, do I switch? Do you? They? My landlady? No, but how do we know about one another for sure?"

"I don't switch, that's for sure, and neither do these 2. They did, you think I'd work with them?"

"And if I did," Doug says, "you think I'd work with you? You're ugly and bald. I'd find a cuter cop."

"Do that. But if you do switch," he says to me, "maybe you should let us know."

"I said no, I don't, but do I know that person well enough to be so sure about everything about her? That's all I'm saying. Forget my landlady, I know almost nothing about her. But Donna I'm positive she doesn't switch or as positive as a person can be without being that person and I'm not that person, I'm not her I mean. What I meant before we started talking about switching was that she's slept with other women's husbands. Some. And single men. But no more than normal I suppose. Normal for a single woman since she still is one and that her sleeping with other men upset me."

"I understand now. Sorry to get it mixed up. Know who was this other man from a year ago?"

"That one I never found out."

"It says here," Doug says holding open a diary, "almost a year ago to today, that you slapped her very hard as you said, 'almost knocking me out. But that blow,' she goes on, 'doesn't bring me down nearly as much as Doc's going does. More later,' but there's nothing else."

"Doc your nickname?"

"That's right, he was a doctor. Of what I'm not so sure. Eyes, somewhere in the head. Eventually around that time he went back to his own country and wife. Donna wouldn't talk about it. Where, I also don't know."

"Which continent?"

"No idea."

"Hemisphere?"

"One of them."

"Was he black, white, yellow, red?"

"She never said. He did phone a few times. That really made me mad. I used to tell her 'You want to meet him, call him yourself or he where you're working that day but don't have him call here.' A few times I had to give her a message because he said it was very important, like he was suddenly detained and if I didn't tell her not to meet him where she was supposed to she'd be standing out for hours in the rain. I could never make out his thick accent. I don't know how she could understand him most times. His English was almost nonexistent and all the languages I know a little of that I tried to use on him he said 'Don't know, no know, can't stand, again more slow,' like that. Usually I had to suggest or guess at a number of possibilities he was trying to tell me to tell her till he finally after a lot of noes or don't knows said yes yes."

"Maybe this Doc comes up in her diaries later on. But there have been others?"

"Several professions. But only 2 I know of in the past year."

"You can give us their phone numbers and addresses?"

"One hasn't told me anything about this but the other I'm sure I'm not even to say to you he doesn't want his name brought in."

"Get it. He's got anything else to hide but leads on your girl, we won't bug him."

I get Thomas's and Louis's phone numbers and addresses.

"I was just reading, from a week ago, how she now wanted you to leave but you wouldn't. What was the trouble?"

"Nothing. It's been great lately. Other than for that verbal spat a few days ago, which was just over this place getting dirty and she not wanting to do her share cleaning up, or at least what

I thought was dirtiness and her share in causing it and cleaning it up, one of those rare very long up periods with us."

"'To leave me,' she says. 'I want A's to leave me.' You're A's?"

"She never called me it or in a letter or message addressed me or referred to me as such, but those are the initials of my 3 names."

"Middle too?"

"Antone, but I never use it initialed or full. I don't even think she knew it, not that it matters here."

"'A's to leave me but he won't go. I want'—scratch marks, few lines crossed out. Arrow pointing to crossed out section and ending in the margin with her tinier almost illegible script saying 'Very illuminative, almost revelatory, why so impetuous dear zerohead to erase the one thing you've written that you thought made the most sense? What did I say here goddamit?' I can't make out what she crossed out, can you?"

"I don't want to see it."

"If it becomes necessary one of these younger guys with better eyes or some photomicrographic machine we have can. 'A's still insists our ridiculationship'—I guess she's coining—"

"I think so. She was a great coiner, obviously even to herself."

"'ridiculationship is weathering when it's out and out not. It's overboard, every man for himself, capsized."

"I still can't understand it. A week ago?"

"To the day. And same page, above it, a week earlier, she says she doesn't enjoy sex with you anymore. 'I don't—'"

"Come on."

"Come on what? Don't read it? I won't if you don't want me to. I can grab why you wouldn't want to hear."

"Read it all you like, out loud or inside, but I just can't believe it."

"It's right here, read it."

"I believe you."

"I could be making it up."

"Why would you?"

"Because I can be a mean s.o.b. like everyone else. Ask them."

"No, you're a saint, Bo, always," Doug says.

"One of the leading saints," other detective says putting down the trash basket he was looking in. "One of the very best," looking in my socks that I left in my shoes when I undressed.

"'I don't enjoy sex with A's anymore though for that matter don't much enjoy it with anyone else much since Doc. Maybe T.' That's her bestfriend's brother you say."

"Thomas Memblaise."

"I have it down here someplace and his number and address."

"Unless there's another T we don't know about."

"Yeah I got it. With Telegrin's. So it could also be him. 'With T it's occas okay maybe because he's much younger than me though I don't see why that should be the case.'"

"I'm sure Thomas is the T she means. He's around 22 or 3 while Telegrin the way he sounded on the phone seems around my age."

"'But with A's I almost always don't like it with most of the time when he's on me, under me, in me, around me, other end of me, all the me's, in the same bed with me, the shower or tub when he wants to scrub or be scrubbed by me, nowhere, no how, no time, no no I don't and don't know how to tell him I don't and that I want him to clear out of here which I know he won't, to be out of my life for good so go A's, leave, please, just get, I said scat, I meant it go. Oh crap.' Then another series of scratched out lines. But nothing about illuminations and revelations this time. But right after that, and I was kidding before. I'm not a mean s.o.b. and I don't think I could be one and I'm now not making that up to win you over, she says you're too good for her. 'He's extremely bright, witty, pretty, young bodied, sexy and all the resty and deserves someone much better than me.'"

"That's a lie."

"You saying I'm lying or her? She? Who lies in their diary?"

"How do I know who does? Maybe everyone, maybe no one. No, certainly one person must have lied in the centuries and centuries of diaries that have been written and she might just be that one. Because what she said's a lie. I'm not extremely this or that or even all that bright, witty, pretty, sexy with a young body and she's probably trying to compensate for some of the harsher possibly untrue things she said about me before because she might actually believe I might try and read all this."

"Could be. Then we come to the entry before last week's where she again wants you to go. She hasn't written much lately, has she. Only short paragraphs compared to her entries from years ago where some run on for pages for individual days."

"I think she was getting tired of her diary."

"Like this one. 8 years ago. Goes on for 6, 7 pages of the same small sized writing she used in the margin before. You never said she was married."

"She never was."

"Says right here. 'My husband.' Though maybe she was being symbolic. She asked him to leave too. Wants a divorce. She does. He won't give it. Says he'll die if he leaves, at least be very lost. She says she can't put up with his morbid melodrama—infantile she calls it also, any man's. Cites his bullshit. Her words. And so on so forth."

Flips the pages. Other detectives are now just listening for the first time. "Aha. She gets the divorce. So she had to have been married. Flew to Quadalodgia to get it, then walked back across the border because of an unexpected ground crew sit-down. All told took a day and a night and 800 in cash plus local fleecing and fare. You didn't know she was married and divorced?"

"Maybe she was still being symbolic."

"Or had a child?"

"She never did."

"What can I say? It's right here. Big bold letters, quarter of a page high in dark red ink and scores of blue exclamation points." Holds the diary page up to me. I see the red and points and turn away.

"You are a highly principled and conscientious guy."

"No I'm not."

"'Gave my tot up for adoption today. Both prearranged. Not the tot but the giving. And it's not a tot for it doesn't toddle but my child. Aide set me straight on that yesterday. In the hospital. 3 days old, both the child and my stay here, visit paid for by adopters and even candy and flowers and a thousand dollars though I've more than adequate birth coverage. I don't feel sad. I don't feel glad. I don't feel—I feel relieved, that's what, and a whit sore from where I was so small I had to be sawed and sewed up. A child would be an obstruction and other things now in my life and career. I asked them not to show it to me or tell me what sex it was but a nurse let on that it hung well as if I'd be happy to hear. Bastard.' This was written months after the divorce so it could have been from someone other than her husband, if 'by husband' and 'divorcing him' wasn't used symbolically. Though how could it have been with that Quadalodgia trip and sudden sitdown? But the baby can't be symbolic. That she had in reality if this diary is on the up and up. But you didn't know any of this."

"I'm surprised to hear of it."

"You don't act surprised."

"But I am. I'm also, both from her being missing and what I'm just now hearing, in the type of semishock I think where one can articulate reasonably well about that shock while still being in it."

"You lived with her for 3 years?"

"And a half."

"Amazing. I bet there are things about my own wife I don't know like that. I bet there are things these guys know about my wife that I don't. I bet."

"All we know," Doug says, "is what you told us, unless Ted knows something you kept from me. She's sweet, petite, gorgeous, gentle, tender, great figure, just 21, rich, compassionate, handy, earthy, man's greatest companion and friend and a terrific wage earner, housecleaner, cook, bottlewasher and joke-teller and great in bed. Sleeps peacefully I mean. Doesn't snore or hog the mattress or covers. And she's also got a great head."

"A great head. And sleeps without disturbing me in bed. That's correct. That's all I ever said. Don't go distorting any of that. Especially her great head. I don't want anyone to know the truth. I'm only kidding and he is too," Bo says to me. "My wife is a prince." They all laugh. "Well it's better than her being a frog or queen. No, I won't say anymore. This place may be tapped. Or a recorder on one of you guys and you might send her a tape of what I said. If it is, I love you sweetheart like no husband has ever loved his mistress or wife from the history of mankind. Need anymore time here, Doug? Ted?"

"If we can keep some of these recent letters to her awhile," Ted says.

"I think so," I say.

"I don't know whose legally they are now or the diaries," Bo says, "but they might help us in finding her. You want to complain, you can. We expect it in fact. I can give you the telephone and name where to. Our own dearly beloved captain."

"No, take whatever you want. Take anything of mine also. My socks."

"I think we'll leave those behind this time."

"You fellows like a beer before you go?"

"Sure, why not? I think I can speak for us all."

"I'm starved," Doug says, "and we were on our way to supper when we stopped off here for what you said would be a minute, so why don't we just leave?"

"Slip it to us on the run then. You can stick it in a paper bag for us, even better."

I give them 3 beers and at the door ask what the chances are of Donna being found.

"Usually if someone's missing and not located from a few hours to 2 days and no ransom note or phonecall's been received. And there's no background of alcoholic blackouts and what's that again, amnesia or even runaways, that person ends up no good and is found from 8 to 10 days and usually in woods 20 or so miles from where she was last seen. If it's a man it's usually 4 to 5 days when he pops up in a lake when the weights on him weren't enough or came off or from his smells in a car trunk at a busy airport."

"Thanks." They go.

Gabe calls. "Where are you? I missed the first bus and you still didn't meet me. Any good news? I sense it."

"Police were just here. I wish it looked better. Maybe she's on overseas assignment. I just thought of that. Her agency's receptionist said no but when I was in the movies Donna could've gotten a call to replace someone and immediately got a plane and left a note for me but took it by mistake or didn't even have time to and the telegram she wired was through some error never sent."

"No. It's the worst, I know now," and breaks down.

"Gabe, you okay? I can't hear you. Try and stop sobbing. I've got to use this phone to call her agent. Take a cab over. I'll pay for it and meet you out front."

"I can't. Pick me up here. In no emotional condition to go to your home alone. I'll be at the middle newsstand if I can hold up or at the drugstore lunch counter directly across."

Curt calls while I'm looking for the agent's number. "How's it going?"

"Awful. Any idea where Donna might be?"

"That's an odd opening right off. No. I wanted to see if you 2 want to see the last show of *Begs* tonight."

"We saw it. She's missing. At least I haven't seen her since she left that movie theater alone Thursday night."

"Thursday? What's your worry? I saw her Friday night."

"Where?"

"Or think I did. Sure. At Bewilderlips. She came in for a quick wine spritzer before she said she was going to meet you to see, that's right, *Begs*. How could I forget? Naturally, if she was leveling with me, you wouldn't want to see it again so soon."

"That was Thursday night."

"No, Thursday night I was to meet you and couldn't, remember?"

"That was Wednesday night. You didn't meet me because you went to a friend's card game."

"That was Thursday. I know because I slashed my hand with my palette knife that day and wore a bandage and most of them joked I was stashing away cards on them in it."

"I'm sorry, that was Wednesday."

"That was Wednesday? I thought it was Thursday because I still had the bandage on when I saw Donna the next night that I thought was Friday and she asked me about it. What's today then, Sunday? Good god, I can't go to the movies tonight. I'm to pick up my daughter at her aunt's house to put her on the train home and I'm already 3 hours late. She'll kill me. Her mother will. All 3 of them. They're all probably calling my apartment now. I don't blame them. I don't want my one kid traveling home so late and when she looks like Gretchen does."

Hangs up. Calls back. "Line's busy. I called her mother and her phone's busy too. What do you mean Donna's missing? She can't be. Since Thursday? No slight, but more to relieve your mind a bit, from what you 2've intimated to me over the past months she's most likely with somebody she conveniently forgot to tell you about or on a field assignment for a few days."

"That's what I'm looking for now, her agent's number, though I'm sure neither of them's the reason."

"Beverly's? I got it right here. I once dated her, Donna and you fixed me up. We went doubles, don't you remember?"

"I forget. Get it."

"It didn't work. I'm looking for it in my address book. We were exact opposites. I revealed everything, she nothing. I thought I had it here. It's in the phonebook."

"She must be unlisted, I looked."

"She gives herself an ironic comical name so only her friends will know it, no strangers. Something to do with agenting. Modeling and agenting. Also a man's first name so no screwball thumbing through the book will also call her just because she's a woman. I know I always don't get it at first and then suddenly get it when I remember the name has something to do with my own work. Clay Pedler. One d. But got to go. Now you got me jumpy. Donna missing, though I know she's all right, what about my daughter? She's such a stubbornbrain and supersensitive she might run out of her aunt's house 2 hours after I didn't show to go to the train station alone. Or even take the train home alone. But it's too late for that type of bravado anymore, too late."

I call Beverly. "Hello. Sorry. I'm unbelievably tired, whoever this is—"

"Beverly, listen—"

"—got back late today from a grueling crosscountry business trip of several sleepless nights and fatiguing days and I can't speak to anyone. Pardon. Neglected to mention this is Beverly on her phone machine speaking. Tell me who you are and your message and after the beep—I mean. Wait for the beep and then give your name and message, which is only a sign of how tired I am, that beep before the mistake, the message, whatever it is, but why am I going on about it for? And I'll get back to you tomorrow midday."

Beep. "Beverly, it's Art. Joanne called you about Donna? If she didn't, I'm calling you now. We're all very worried. Don't be alarmed, there hasn't been an accident, but Donna hasn't been seen or heard from since late Thursday night. Though maybe there was an accident. Hadn't thought of that till now. I'm sure the police checked into it, but maybe they haven't and she was taken to a hospital and had no identification on her or lost it during the accident—her purse. She was carrying a purse that night, I just remembered that now too and didn't tell it to the police and they didn't ask and maybe that's why we don't know where she is and she hasn't been home. For you see, we went to a movie, she left early and never got home, though she said she was heading right home. Is she out on assignment? Overseas? That's what I called for. Your receptionist said no. Please call me first thing before anyone tomorrow to confirm. Many thanks. Bye."

I phone the hospital near us. Man says "There were plenty of women brought in that night after the time you say and age. What's her name and address?"

"You missed my point. If she had her name and address on her I would've been contacted by you or the police by now. What I'm interested in is if any woman, fairly young, tall, not fairly tall but considerably tall for a woman, 6 feet and she—"

"Wait wait. Young. 21?"

"31."

"Tall. 6. Okay."

"Looks like a fashion model. Is one. Short dark hair, curly, thin figure, very attractive, like that, tiny waist and flat breasts and long legs."

"Wait wait wait. Short. Dark. Curly. Thin. Tiny. Pretty. Flat. Long. Yeah."

"And wearing blue denims—jeans, jacket and shirt and possibly a red purse, was brought in—"

"Wait. Blue. Red. Go on."

"Was brought in Thursday night after 10 without any identification on her."

"Thurs. 10. Let's see. Where's the list? Hanna, where's Thusday's admittance list? Hanna? Les, where'd Hanna go? Lester? Hold it. They all went. Turn your back, zoom, out for coffee or whatever they're out for altogether as if I didn't like coffee either and should man the phones for them all alone. There's Carlos. Where's Les and Hanna? For the admittance list for Thursday. Thanks loads. Right under my nose he says. Piles of papers someone else put there right under my nose above the list but okay. Thursday, after 10. Yeah, there was one, but she died. Young but wasn't anything like yours could have been. Heavy, that's the main difference. Yours could have gained weight with a crash gorging since you last saw her, even in a day, but not that much. But she was very thin to begin with you said and a model, so 50 pounds since then? No, though it could have been 150 with this one she was so big and what she died from. Her weight. Couldn't run. Someone was chasing her. She tried, got a heart attack and died. Also 6 feet or over and no one knows why no identification she was so well groomed and dressed. Maybe the chaser got her pocketbook after she dropped, but that's impossible all that gained weight in one day for your friend. Only other n.i. that night was a man. You come up with his name we'll be thrilled to give you him, wrapped in ribbons. A nuisance. Already socked one guard's eye out who had to be hospitalized here and says he's John Doe, but the original one they named all the others after. Actually we can't give you him as soon as he's healed he gets tried for jail under his alias. Where can you be reached? Any other n.i. comes in near to what yours looks like or I hear around, I'll give you a buzz."

I go downstairs and tape a note over the building's mailboxes: Anyone seen Donna Akers, apt. 4W (tall fashion model) since late last Thursday night, please let me know. Art Alimin (apt. 4W, tel: 324-1279). Thanks

I cab to the terminal. Gabe's not at Information. I go into the drugstore and look around. "Excuse me," I say to the counterman, "but have you seen—"

"Waiter, get me another coffee?"

"Just a minute, ma'am. I'm talking to somebody."

"Don't just no minute ma'am to me, man. I got a bus to catch and my money ready to pay you, so let me have it."

"Do it," I say. "I can wait."

"Why? Just by the way she spoke to me she deserves nothing first."

"Better than have her raise hell I'd think."

"You're right, what am I doing?" and pours her another coffee, moves the cream pitcher and sugar dispenser near to her and takes her check.

"What're you think you're doing with that?"

"Writing up another coffee."

"35 cents more for a coffee when I already had a cup plus tax? I should get this one gratis."

"That's not our policy."

"It's the policy over all the country. I know. I've traveled."

"But it's not ours. You had a sandwich or even a soup with it maybe, that'd been different."

"I had a coffee, way overpriced, that should be enough. Come on, don't lick the master's ass. Forget you poured the second cup, who's to know?"

"I will. I'm also my own man but my superior over there—see her?" pointing to a woman behind the cigarette counter. "She might have seen, because she sees and memorizes everything. She spies for the company and got god knows how many workers fired, and later when she checks my checks she'll ask how come no charge for that lady's second cup? That alone I can get fired for. You don't want to pay for this, no hard feelings, I understand," and puts her check down without having written on it and picks the cup off the saucer.

"But you already poured it. Where you'll dump it, in the sink?"

"Back in the urn then."

"That's a health violation. Who wants to drink coffee poured back. Leave it here."

"You'll pay for it?"

"I'll pay for nothing goddamnit," and she tries taking the cup from him and some of it spills on her hand. "You sonofabitch, now look what you done."

"Who tried to take what out of my hands, me?"

"Excuse me," I say to them. "I don't want to interfere but this is very important also. Have you seen—" to him.

"Wait a minute. I'm burning. This asslicker just burnt me."

"I did not. You tried grabbing the cup from me because you wouldn't pay for it and when I was holding it back—"

"You mean I don't get any sympathy from you? You're not even going to say a sorry for this?"

"I was burned a couple drops by you too you know and you don't hear me screaming for apologies. You're lucky I don't sic the cops on you."

"You bastard," and she reaches for the saucer.

"Don't!" I say.

She swipes the saucer to the floor and grabs the sugar dispenser.

"Duck!"

Does but the dispenser hits him in the head. Woman jumps off the stool, picks up a valise and runs out. Woman selling cigarettes drops behind the candy case. Counterman falls against the cash register, chin clipping the shelf as he goes down, $4.80 ringing up and drawer opening. He's on the floor. I look over the counter at him. Eyes closed, blood from his nose, cup still spinning by his hand. Someone grabs my elbow and I think it's Gabe and turn around but it's a bus terminal policeman saying "What the hell you do to Rees?"

"Nothing, it was a lady. Hit him with that sugar thing there and ran out of here with a valise."

"What lady? I just came in here and nobody ran out when I did so this must've just happened. I looked in 10 seconds ago and Rees was fine."

"You didn't see them arguing?"

"Didn't see or hear anyone arguing. Stay put till I get my head collected and help for him."

"It was a lady with a suitcase like he says," the cigarette woman says. "I don't think him also. Least I didn't see him come in with her, but she was the one who threw it okay. Her face I won't forget so fast in a million years. Rees, you okay? Get up, you got work to do, customers are waiting."

"Don't say that," the policeman says. "He might be dying down there."

"I wasn't serious. I thought maybe I could shock him up."

Policeman goes around the counter and puts his ear to Rees's mouth. "Sonofagun. I don't know how hard he was hit with this but he doesn't sound like he's breathing. Gwen, run outside on the emergency phone and tell them to rush with an ambulance."

"Who'll mind my register?"

"Get your assistant there."

"He'll steal me silly."

"No I won't," the assistant says.

"Then get him to go to the phone but one of you rush."

"Go to the yellow emergency phone in the terminal and call for an ambulance," she says.

"Where is it?"

"By the bar. I know you know where that is. Then by the bar."

He runs out, comes right back. "What do I tell them again?"

"I'll do it," a customer says and she runs out.

"Listen," I say to the policeman, "I don't like asking this right now but I'm supposed to meet—"

"Just stay put."

"But this man's old the one I'm to meet and a wreck because his daughter might be dying."

"Don't give me no stories. Even if it's true, I maybe have my own dying here and got to find some things out first. Rees?"

Rees opens his eyes. "Oh Christ."

"Rees, how are you? It's Stew. Don't move. But is this guy involved in who did it to you?"

"Who? What? Stew? Move? No. Not Stew. Never saw him before."

"Then I can go?"

"Rees, stay awake. I'm Stew. The bus terminal guard. We both know I didn't do it. But this is a man who might be with the lady who threw the sugar pourer at you. Look at him. Over the counter on your right. Stick your head way more over the counter you," to me. "Now, he with the lady who hit you?"

"No. Don't know who he is. Who his he. Is he. Hit me. What pourer. What my doing back. My here, head, mouth of flood."

"Rest, buddy. And you—Gwen will give that lady's description to the police. Leave your name and where they can get you just so if she's caught, not that she will in these crowds."

"I know you'll be all right, Rees," I say, "take care." Closes his eyes. I give a napkin with my name and phone number to Stew and go to the cigarette counter. "By the way, did you see—"

"Please, I'm too shaken now to answer questions," holding her head.

"This'll take a second. He's an elderly man. I'm worried about him. Almost my father-in-law. Grayhaired but very tall and powerfully built for his age and probably dressed in a tie and white shirt but clean overalls or dungarees and he's—"

"Please I said. Don't provoke me. It's been a tough night."

"Package of spearmint," a woman says.

"16 cents."

"What happened there, robbery?"

"You have a penny?"

Gives her a penny, gets a dime change. "What was it, holdup?"

"You didn't see? There's a body behind there. Take a look. Rees, our counterman, he's alive. What else ever happens around here nights and days? Crazies, maniacs. Worse to worse each year. No real police when you need them. What was I thinking? It's worse to worse from week to week, killers and thieves. Witch who did it she's probably already back in the woodwork here to pop out and bop somebody tomorrow. Rees and I should feel lucky we're still alive enough to even have come in today. Now women are knocking down big men with clubs for cups of coffee. Little kids next will be stabbing me with icepicks for nickel sticks of gum. He'll be all right. Though I bet he'll now want 2 sick days off and to replace him we'll get the world's swiftest thief. Sometimes I swear I don't like this life anymore, here or where I live for 30 years, but at least I can tell myself I'm not selling babies or illegal drugs and guns."

From a phone in the terminal I call the police station and tell one of Bo's associates that Donna also had a red cloth purse when we went to the movie that night.

"Sure she didn't leave it in the theater?"

"She carried her keys in it so how would she think she'd get in?"

"When you leave something you obviously don't think. Unless she wanted to leave it and as you say I'm sure she didn't. But that could be the reason she didn't get in. Her keys in the purse which she might have left in the theater. And then something happened when she walked back to the theater to get her purse let's say. Ask the manager if he found it. I'll write down here red cloth purse."

"Even if the manager found it or person who cleans up, I doubt they'd return it. It's a cheap theater. I'm sure they don't get paid much or care what the customers think of them or their trap and they also could make a few bucks splitting whatever they find under the seats every night."

"No harm in asking. You'd be surprised, people can be very honest. But that's it?"

"What about my neighbors? You speak to any of them? She could've gotten in that night and somebody saw her, maybe being dragged off or followed in and is just waiting to be questioned, thinking that if he or she's not then nothing's wrong."

"We haven't yet not that we haven't thought about it. But good idea, good figuring. Don't worry though, 3 trained heads with a combined total of 45 years experience are a lot better than one novice one and everything that's to be done is being taken care of or ready to."

My note's been taken down from above the mailboxes. Top left ragged corner of it left with a strip of tape over it. I ring all the tenants' bells. Nobody answers or rings back. Let myself in and from the ground floor hallway yell upstairs "Hello. Hello everybody, please listen. I know it's late but nothing could be more urgent for me now and maybe for all of us. I'm a desperate man. Just yelling upstairs at you at this hour proves it. It's Art from apartment 4W. Did anyone see my note about Donna Akers before? I left it over the mailboxes. Someone tore it off. Well you all know Donna. She's a model, my friend and roommate. Tall. 6 feet or more. Slimly built. Very pretty, dark hair, curly, cut short, a very pleasant person. I know she knows the Bluds in 4E right across the hall from us and she's spoken to just about all of you from time to time as I have. You've also seen her face in magazines, mostly fashion, and a few newspapers and reproduced on billboards. Some of you have commented on seeing these and a couple times in television ads. Recently. Mostly in soap and car spots, Donna sudsing her legs and toes in a heartshaped bathtub or standing on top of a mesa in a desert with a new bubbletopped van. You've commented to me about that one particularly—how the van got up there, was it by helicopter?—the Granges for one, and Rex Salvio in 2W. Well she's missing. Listen. Hello?" Nobody's opened the door that I can hear. "Did anyone tear up that note I wrote saying Donna's been missing since late Thursday night? It's true. I was in a movie with her. Theater. The Coliseum. This Thursday night. Last. She left early. I'm sorry if I've awakened any of you or am keeping you from going to sleep but I have to go on. Donna didn't like the movie. Hello? I thought I heard someone, a door opening, did I? Well she left early and said she'd see me home. She never got home. Or maybe she did but she wasn't home when I got there about an hour later. The police are looking for her now. They think foulplay. I don't know what to think. I'm almost too panicked to think. I'm scared as hell for her that's for sure and I'll do anything to get her back short of putting her life in more danger if that's what it's in. This is nothing my yelling upstairs at this hour waking or keeping everyone up as much as it must be to most of you. Nothing compared to what I might do such as knocking on your doors at all hours tonight if I think that's necessary to see if you know anything about where she might be. So answer me now, please, to avoid my having to knock on your doors tonight or worse, did anyone see Donna get home? That's all the note's about. Did anyone see her coming in, going out, on the street, Thursday night, sometime after 10? Was she with a friend? Man or woman? Anyone know? Could describe? That night. Even any day or night since then if you've seen her anywhere in this city or actually anywhere since it doesn't have to be in this building or on the block. Hello? This is Art from apartment 4W for those of you just listening in and I'm yelling because I'm desperately as I said in need of help and worried about the health, life and whereabouts of Donna Akers of 4W and sooner we the police and I get some lead on her the better chance we'll have of finding her if it is foulplay, if it's not too late. So can anyone give me some information, anything, if you saw her, please open your door and let me know, that's all I ask. If it's nothing and she left of her own accord or is vacationing or away on location working, I'll apologize to each of you personally same day I find that out, though I absolutely or almost don't believe it's any of those which is why I'm acting this way now. So I'm ready to listen to you. I will keep quiet now and just listen."

Nobody unlocks or opens his door. Least I can't hear anything. I walk upstairs. All the doors are closed. 2 to a floor. I go past my apartment to the fifth floor. 2 doors here are closed too. I look at the peepholes of both. Sometimes I can catch light through the hole indicating someone's watching but the holes here are dark. They could be watching from a dark room. I don't hear anyone behind the doors. I stand still. Hold my breath. No sounds. One step, stop, quickly hold my breath, thinking I can catch them off guard, no one stirs. I go up the last flights, unlatch the door. I hadn't thought about the roof before. And the police? Maybe her body's up here. Of course not no, god knows, impossible, but every possibility has to be tried. I enter the roof and look around. It's very dark. I wait a minute for my eyes to adjust to the dark but they don't. 2 minutes. Eyes still don't. I'll need a flashlight. Moon's barely a sliver. Clouds, only a few stars out. I go to my apartment and look for a flashlight. We've 2, pocketlight and larger one. While I'm looking I think this is the first time in 4 nights I didn't think Donna would or might be here when I came in. It could mean I've given up too. Have? I have. Haven't. I don't have a flashlight. I thought I did with the few tools we have but they're not here or haven't been for a while. Gabe? Probably took what might have been the last bus home, tired of waiting for me, didn't want to stay with me, always objected to our living unmarried together, couldn't afford a hotel. I must remember to call him later. Tomorrow. What was I thinking of before?

Flashlight. I ring 4E. No answer. Knock on the door. No sound. Pound on it. Pound for a minute on it. I'm almost sure they're home. Sure they're home. They've children. The Bluds only entertain now, never visit people's homes or even take long walks alone together because of their 3 young children. People don't understand that, they've said. We've lost friends because of it. We don't trust sitters and can't take the children with us and people also don't want them there and think their visits and dinners at our house have to be repaid by us to theirs and that we're avoiding their homes, even our own relatives. Besides it's too late for them. Donna's sat for them several times to give them a break and play with their boys, only sitter they've allowed. He works days and she gets up even earlier with the youngest 2 so usually goes to sleep an hour before him. Then I hear shuffling. Peephole opens. Light behind it. All I can see.

After a half minute I say "Yes it's me."

"What is it?"

"You didn't hear me from downstairs?"

"We heard you. Who couldn't? Across the street and way through our apartment into the backyard and beyond they heard you, not to say in Mary's dreams. We're sorry about Donna if it's true."

"Did you tear down my note?"

"Never saw a note."

"Neither of you?"

"Nor the boys. Nor my mother out-of-town. Nobody we know."

"You don't know anything about Donna, see anyone that night? Seen her since then? She used to be very friendly with you both."

"And we used to be friendly with her too, though never so late. She knew we had work to do early and the kids. The oldest is only in kindergarten. Morning session. That we don't enjoy commotions of any sort or loud music past 10."

"I know that too. Once 10 came I always kept my voice and music low. And that your 2 youngest sons get you both up a few times every night for water or bad dreams or to make pee. I don't want to bother anyone."

"You're desperate, we heard. It's urgent. Your message got across, Art. You've an effective way of presenting yourself, not that we're so coldhearted where we aren't affected by what you say. But we're too exhausted to think about Donna now. Coherently I mean, constructively I'm saying, so let us get back to bed.

Mary and I. You too if you want to. You probably need the rest."

"Can you loan me a flashlight? We had 2 but seem to have misplaced them. That's more what I originally rang your bell for. I want to check all the connected roofs. People go up there rarely. A body could get stuffed and lost behind some roof rubbish. It must sound ridiculous."

"I can empathize your thinking her disappearance is extremely important, but we don't believe it happened in any of the ways you say. Let's face it, you 2 had problems. Emotional. Marital if you were married. Sexual from what I heard. Constitutional from what we could surmise and maybe congenital, not that we'll ever get that close to you to know. Donna told Mary and confidentially, Mary told me. We talk. That's how we last. Don't tell either of them I told you though. Individually you 2 are stimulating and attractive and a delight to have around but as a pair I could never see where it worked. I'm repressing a lot less than I generally do because I want to help you and get some shuteye myself. Our deduction grounded on our logical apprizement and discussions of what we see as the facts or those that have diverted into our personal purview is that she disappeared because she didn't know how to say goodbye to you since she knew you'd never accept a simple or complex goodbye from her and wouldn't say one yourself and leave her the apartment alone. She told us."

"Told you that's why she left?"

"That you wouldn't. Told Mary I mean and Mary of course confidentially to me. Most likely reason she hasn't reached you is she feels she needs to be completely free from you a few weeks to resist your pleading that she return."

"Why wouldn't she contact you or one of her best friends?"

"Maybe afraid we'll spill the beans to you where she is."

"She could've just said to you 'I'm away and safe but won't say where I am.'"

"Too cryptic for Donna. You know she's plainspoken and since she can't speak plainly to you or us about this she assumes, I'm assuming, we know she's okay and why she left. She's told us, I figure she's told others how she feels about you."

"She'd leave without clothes? Nothing?"

"Nothing you can be certain she didn't leave with."

"You know that to say?"

"I'm presuming. Naked? No. But what were you saying? I told you I'm tired, confused. I'd even at this stage, in the worst of crises, risk a joke—which this wasn't, not a crisis, only maybe not a joke. Begin again. Donna didn't take any clothes?"

"She probably never even got back here after the movie."

"You comb through her closets, luggage, drawers and shoes?"

"Not closely. Didn't think I had to. Besides, I don't know all her clothes. Maybe the previous day she gave half her clothes away and bought a new wardrobe but left it at the stores. She never tells me these things and why should she? She knows I'm not interested unless there's an interesting story involved. Now I would be but then not. And some things I see her in I think she just bought or borrowed and she tells me she's worn it with me 20 times."

"Her bankbook, checkbook, passport?"

"Look for it? No, the police did. All her papers except what she had with her are there."

"You know all her papers? Clothes no but papers yes? Come on, who does? In 12 years I don't know most of Mary's papers nor Mary mine. We're better off that way. I've compiled enough in those years to fill 5 file cabinets. Ask me what kind of insurance policy she has. That I should know. I don't. If she has any? I forget. Her citizenship? Was she born here, overseas? Give me a minute to think about that. See? And I'm not joking. What about Donna's personal belongings? Jewelry, rings. Ones especially you bought. Check those?"

"Police did."

"They know what to look for? They've lived with her, seen her take them on and off?"

"Maybe they know what should be there but isn't. As for the jewelry, only thing I gave her was a waist chain that takes a little key on her keyring to get off. Rest are from previous relationships or family relics or giveaways from her modeling jobs, but I'll check."

"Her contraceptive device. It's in her or she keeps it in a case?"

"Case. I'll look." I run back and look in the medicine chest. "Case is there."

"You look inside?"

"I shook it."

"You're not saying that so you don't have to go back?"

"And the necessary accessories, plunger, tube. All there."

"Then unless she has another one she wouldn't I don't think leave without that. And her not being cryptic, she wouldn't want you to assume she has. She never did when she went on location for several days, did she?"

"Even when she stayed away for a night, she always took the case with her. Also the plunger though not always the tube. That one I think she had 2. When she came back and unpacked and if I was home at the time I'd usually shake the case soon as she put it back in the medicine chest to see if anything was inside. Wasn't, I'd sulk. She'd ask why, I'd get gloomier but wouldn't reply."

"The case could've been empty for you those times or for later that night. Her birth control device. Donna's."

"Mary, you're next to Tod? You've any idea where or why Donna might've gone?"

"Please be quiet, Art," someone from downstairs yells.

"Yes," someone from upstairs. "It's late. Turn it off like she says."

"Have any of you—"

"No."

"No."

Their doors slam.

"Then who tore down my note?"

"An outsider perhaps," someone from the first or second floor. "They can throw pint bottles through my window same day my bike's ripped off its inch thick lock out front and mailbox is jimmied in, they can tear down your note. So go to sleep, Art, tomorrow's work."

"Do as he says. You too, Tod. You'll be in a stupor all day if you don't."

"Night, Art."

"Flashlight first?"

"Oh Jesus, give up. She's gone because she didn't want to

stay, no matter what's not missing from your place. It's only that we've missed unriddling this but don't keep up a whole house for it. They'll think you insane. You'll get evicted for it. We'll sign the commitment and eviction papers, 9 different apartments and the super will. Show some humor, courage, even self-reproach."

"Flashlight."

"Mary?"

Door opens, chain on it. Flashlight head can't fit through. Closes, opens, chain's off. Mary hands me the flashlight, closes the door, chains it.

"I don't know if you can know how bad I feel about her," I say.

"Oh we don't. He's saying he doesn't think we don't. Laugh. The worst thing is if anything did actually happen to Donna and all our conclusions are wrong, we're wondering if it wasn't you."

"That's not so," Tod says.

"Yes it is so. Don't lie. We spoke."

"You don't have to worry about me."

"I don't," Tod says.

"We do too. Why you think we're being so precautious here? Maybe not that precautious anymore by telling you how much. But one thing or the other, you've proven yourself bedbugs either by your having done something to Donna or your reaction to her vanishing. Both, you're crossed off our list."

"I'll return this."

"Not tonight," Tod says. "Leave it by the door."

"I won't even make a noise putting it up against it. I'll leave it in the middle of the mat."

"Middle of the mat someone might kick it going past. Leave it flat up against the door. Don't worry about the extra little noise and next time before you ring or knock phone first." Peephole closes.

I go to the roof, look around with the light. Old crates, rolls of old tarpaper and empty cans of roofing cement, bricks, planks, sheetrock, abandoned plants, liquor and beer bottles, exposed garbage in blighted bags, toppled over tv antenna and crumpled up ones from 20 years ago, bottom part of a milk carton with milk, cat meowing a few roofs away. Night, not much city light, planes high up like dots dawdling different ways, seemingly the same few stars, none recognizable, green and red flashing lights of a helicopter passing looking like an interviewee's description in the news this week of a sighted UFO above a nearby street. Bridges, other boroughs, another state. Siren goes off below by accident or someone breaking into a car. I walk along the other roofs with the flashlight and look around. Siren continues, cat accompanies me. I stop, he or she does too. Pet it. Curls its long tail round my ankle or almost. Pick it up. Yowls, scratches my thumb as it jumps out of my arms. "Stop thief," someone yells from the street, "my car."

Down on my knees shaking my fists to the sky "Donna, goddamn you, whatever, whoever, however it is, did it, happened, ah shit, oh crap, christalmighty, where are you, is she, Donna Akers, anybody, I mean it I mean it, please let me know."

"Who's that there yelling?" from a top floor terrace across the backyards.

Up, "Must've been a car being robbed on the street."

"I'm talking to you, on the roof."

"Me, it's okay, I live here, thought I heard a prowler, came to see what's what."

"No you're not."

"Beg your pardon?"

His big dogs barking, spotlight suddenly on me concentration camp size. "Get off before I call the cops."

"Just 2 more roofs to go. It's actually our cat. Prowler too but cat ran away up the fire escape. You can't dim that while we talk? And the dogs, how can you hear me? You see—I said you see, my little kid's in a tizzy, wailing, keeping us up, won't go to sleep. It was a gift from his—"

"See this? I got a gun."

"Excuse me?"

"Heel. I said heel. I said you see this gun? I got one."

"I'm sorry, I can't."

"Believe me it is. Now get off."

"Wait I want to level with you. Should've done that first. You seem like a kind man. At first I didn't think you'd understand.

It's actually my woman friend here. Maybe you heard me scream. That 'I mean it I mean it' help before. Sure you did. What got you out here. I admit I went a bit off my head. Well she—"

"I won't give you but 3."

Possibly because of the spotlight I can't see the gun but I leave. Latch the roof door, flashlight up against the Bluds' door and key in my lock. Cat walks between my legs, comes back, stays there. Thought it was still on the roof and I give it a shove down the hall. Slides first then knocks over the flashlight as it scampers past and upstairs. I stand the light against the door again, go in mine and lock it. Cat scratches on it, meows. Open. Hesitates before it darts in. I have my foot out, trip it, grab it by its neck and throw it into the hall. "Go home."

"Please Art," Tod says through his door, "no more."

I let it in. Flashlight's fallen or knocked over again, rolled off the mat into the middle of the hallway floor, but I leave it alone.

In the kitchen I tear a newspaper into shreds and put them in a cardboard box, fill a cereal bowl with water and another with raw eggs beaten up with burglarized rolls. Pulverized rolls for it's the bedroom that's been burglarized, which I can see through the kitchen door. Dumbwaiter I'm standing beside which the burglar might have come through. Could still be there. If the elevator inside was moving I'd hear it squeak. Press my ear against the door but there's no sound from the shaft or breath. Bedroom drawers pulled out, things, clothes, stockings, undies, socks, hankies, jewelry box, letters on the floor. My watch on the dresser gone from where I put it when I came back from the morgue. 50 dollars or so I keep in an envelope in the top dresser drawer. I look for the burglar in the apartment, keeping my ears cocked to the dumbwaiter, carrying a brass candlestick by its top end, candle I threw against the kitchen wall. "Sonofabitch, bastard, you mother, goddamnit," I yell stomping through the rooms and hall, "I've had enough, this is too much, if you're here you better say so and come out and give up our stuff and leave peacefully through the front door. I'll let you, or else I'm going to break your head in with this candlestick if you don't goddamnit, I'll do it you mother, bastard, sonofabitch," throwing open closet doors and smashing and stabbing clothing and what might be behind it with the candlestick, looking under the couch but first sitting hard on it, behind the shower curtain which falls brackets and all but which I first throw Donna's hairblower at and swat right and left, utility closet where the ironing board looking like a burglar comes down on me and which I swing the candlestick at and put a hole through the louver door, inside the slightly ajar kitchen sink cabinet big enough to fit a normal sized man crouched up and the cat bounds out. Then I knock on the dumbwaiter door. Only place he could still be if he's here. Other hand stretches over and takes a carving knife out of the dish drainer. Cat runs through my legs, comes back, stays there playing with my cuff, I kick it away. Its 2 bowls on the floor untouched. "Eat, go on and eat you dumb mutt." Siren never stops. Dogs did when their master said heel and now start up again but immediately stop at his command hush. It's happened before, not the burglary at least to me, but the car siren alarm and often the dogs. Siren usually lasts all night, even after the police come, who won't tamper with the car hood, private property, they can get in trouble, "Want to complain there's a special phone number for anti-noise," they've told me, "though they close at 5." Neighbors on the street screaming "Turn it off, who's that horn?" I can hear from way back here but it'll probably go on till the battery dies or driver gets in the car the next morning few minutes to 8 when both parking sides have to vacate their spots for heavy traffic and the sanitation sweeper and garbage and private carting trucks. I knock on the dumbwaiter door this time with the candlestick end. No bolt on the door. Was one once. We thought of getting it replaced. I said I would. What I say and what I do. A neighbor, Mary, warned us when she saw our dumbwaiter door boltless. That's right, she did say they'd been burglarized once through the dumbwaiter before we moved in, bolt left unbolted on their door, and attempts on other tenants, I don't know how successfully, Rex Salvio twice, the whoseawhatsits right above Rex on the third floor. I knock on the door harder this time, much, denting it and the candlestick end. Face it. Open it. Nobody's in there anyway. But somebody could be or have been. Only way the burglar could've come in the apartment and left. Front door was locked, all our windows sheer drops, no fire escape except for the apartments facing the street which we're not one. A key. He could've gotten it from some place. Donna's purse, her address inside the purse, not so much gotten the purse off of Donna but from out of the street. Even if he had come in through the front door key or not and then locked it he could still be hiding in there. Holding my breath I hear breathing in the shaft.

"Donna? No of course not. But Donna you in there? No don't be silly no." But in a hurry to get her things. Why through the dumbwaiter then? Not through it but now sitting in it so not to see me. No, dumb thought Donna in the dumbwaiter hiding from me. For one thing she's afraid of heights. Another it's too absurd. Heights yes but not of me. But the breathing if it was. Could've been air breezing down the shaft from somewhere. I know nothing about currents in shafts. Could also be Mary or Tod on the other side of the shaft behind their dumbwaiter door listening in close to me thinking what could he be up to next? "Mary? Tod? That you? Either both? One of your boys? Kevin, Jonah, Ross?" Even if it were I don't think they'd answer me now and the 2 youngest boys can't say anything yet but dada and ma. "Mary, Tod, Jonah, my apartment's been burglarized, I think the burglar's in the dumbwaiter elevator right behind our doors if it wasn't you breathing just before. Was it? One of you? Even if it was he could still be in there. If it's Ross or Kev get your mother or father, your dada or ma, get them. Only way the burglar could've gotten in my place. No he could've gotten in with a key if he got it out of Donna's purse or through some ruse off the super's keyrack. But open up. No, just listen and tell me if you hear breathing in there, but don't open for he might still be in the dumbwaiter elevator on our floor waiting for us with a gun or knife or that stuff they spray in your face, mace. Another thing is bolt your dumbwaiter door, quick."

I phone the Bluds. No answer. Hang up, again, no answer.

"You, if you're in there—whatever, forget it. If you are, tough crap, you're done, I'm phoning the police."

Phone's beside the dumbwaiter and I dial the police, other hand pressed against the dumbwaiter door, not that a good kick or shoulder shove with his hands or feet braced against the Bluds' door couldn't get him out. But coming out that way I could get him with the candlestick or knife, not that I should count on myself using one of those. Policeman answers and I tell him I've been burglarized and he asks my name and address and says a car will be over when it can.

"I'd hope sooner because the burglar might still be in the dumbwaiter elevator right behind my dumbwaiter door."

"He get in that way?"

"Maybe. My front door was locked when I came in and I don't see much of a possibility where he could've gotten the keys. He could've come through the basement where the dumbwaiter begins or through someone's apartment and into their dumbwaiter elevator and up to my place. I don't know what else has happened in the building. The basement might've been broken in. That's happened before. Maybe several apartments have been robbed and the tenants don't even know it yet, having slept right through it. That happened to my uncle once, wallet from under the pillow his head was on. I know I called everyone out from the hallway before and nobody answered. Maybe my dumbwaiter door's not the only one to have no bolt on it or one of the other tenants left the bolt or hook on theirs off. But half the things I assume to be so aren't so maybe it's my imagination again steering me wrong."

"That was stupid. Of you because who keeps no latches or bolts on their dumbwaiter doors? You should all know better. If you don't or can't those damn dumbwaiters should be outlawed. They still should, with kids being pushed or falling down them, dogs and cats."

"I know it was stupid. I was going to put one on but didn't. We have no kids or pets. But what should I do now? He might be in there, just a few feet away."

"Oh this is beautiful. I'm coming on about how indignant I am when same time you're saying some bum behind an unbolted door who's probably overhearing your part might be ready to pounce out on you with any weapon he chooses. Go slow. Don't bother him. Listen to me. Let him go. Best thing—only—is to grab your keys and leave without your shoes even if you haven't got them on and cross the street and wait there a little further up the block so the burglar coming out of your building won't know you're you. Car will be right over quicker than I said before and meet them out front. He leaves before they get there watch where he goes but don't stop him or look obvious or follow."

I hang up, hear the elevator squeaking. Someone could be sending their garbage to the basement where they'll then go down, if they're considerate, and take the bags off and stick them in the basement garbage cans. Super brings them to the street in the morning. Tenants have done that. Not at this hour. Super usually rings our bells for the garbage at 8. I open the door. Elevator's descending but too dark in the shaft to see it and if I could I still wouldn't be able to see if there's garbage or a man on it because of the elevator roof.

"Hey, this is Art, from 4W, anyone using the elevator, sending their garbage down?" Wouldn't think so since I don't see any light from an apartment where the door would be open, though could be that someone's sending the garbage down in the dark. Because they're undressed. "I'll say it again, whoever's using the elevator or riding it you have to tell me now."

Nobody answers. I grab the ropes and stop the elevator from moving. I feel someone tugging on it. I know the feeling. When I sent down garbage on other days and someone didn't know I was using the dumbwaiter and pulled on the rope to bring the elevator to their floor.

I yell down the shaft "I want my pocketwatch you, I want her jewelry back too. I want my money back. That watch is my only family heirloom, the one thing I really cherish and own. One material thing. I got it from my father after he died. He got it from my mother's father on their wedding day who got it before that from my mother's grandfather. My grandfather did, who was given it by my greatgrandfather on his deathbed who got it from his father or father-in-law. It could even go back further than that. My parents didn't know but the watch is maybe 200 years old. I'm not saying this is an incentive for you to keep it but to warn you how far I'll go to get that watch back. And my money from the top dresser drawer is all I have except for a few bucks in my wallet. Give it back. About 50 dollars. I want every cent of it. I can't afford to be robbed. That watch by the way I want to give to my son one day if I have one but that's my business who I give it to if I don't have a boy or girl, but it's not going to you. I'll hold these ropes all day if I have to but it's not going to you. Now turn them over. The money, jewelry and watch."

I knock on the Bluds' dumbwaiter door, keep knocking and yelling "Tod, Mary, how can you stay in there?" while I hold both ropes. Nobody answers.

"People, tenants, there's a burglar in the dumbwaiter elevator who I've caught. I've got hold of the ropes. Don't open your dumbwaiter door if you live on the third floor and below because he might be facing it. The Bluds and fifth floor you can. Just open and look down and you'll see I'm not crazy but right. I can't see the burglar though maybe I could if one of you, Bluds or fifth floor tenants, shined a flashlight down the shaft. The police I've called and they're coming. And my friend's jewelry, you down there, most are heirlooms also, some going back as far as my pocketwatch and probably more. Her mother gave them to her, her grand and greatgrands too. I want them. I'm keeping them for her. The portable tv I can see from here is also gone. It's always on our dresser, but it's yours if you want new as it is but the money and especially my pocketwatch and her heirloom jewelry I want back now."

"I don't have your jewelry."

"What? What're you talking about? I saw her jewelry box on the bedroom floor."

"I dropped the box when I heard you coming in, didn't have time to grab up any of it."

"Then my money and watch."

"I never saw them. You came in and caught me at it too fast."

"They're gone from the dresser top and top dresser drawer where they always are, don't bullshit me. That only proves or tends to you're probably lying about the jewelry too."

"All right, I'm lying, but not about the jewelry, I swear. Let go of the ropes and I'll leave the watch and money on the basement floor."

"You'll just take off from the basement with them to the street."

"Let's not argue but strike a bargain. You want your goodies back and I want to get home."

"I don't have to strike anything. The police are coming. I got the ropes. You're stuck."

"I can cut the ropes. I might get hurt but it can't be that much of a drop."

"I think only the ropes will fall but the elevator car won't."

"The car will. I have out my knife."

"I'm not sure. It might be held by the cable. But don't try it. The shaft's narrow. I forget what's at the bottom. Pulleys maybe or whatever's at the opposite end of pulleys. Cable spool maybe. It could be sharp. You can get yourself killed."

"All that's below this is dirt floor." Lights a match, it drops a few feet and goes out. Lights another, it drops about the same distance and goes out. "I can't see but I know it's only dirt. You want your money and watch, let me lower myself down. If not I'm cutting the ropes and if the car doesn't fall or I see I'm caught I'll smash your watch against the wall and tear your money to confetti."

"Leave the watch and money on the ledge at the bottom of the next door you pass and I'll let you go all the way down."

"Okay. Tv's mine though. Jewelry you know I don't have."

"I'm not so sure."

"I don't. Now make it quick. Let go of the ropes."

"But how can I know you'll leave the money and watch on the ledge if I can't see them? You have a flashlight?"

"I've matches. I'll leave the whole book lit on the ledge by the money and watch but not that close where the money will get burned."

"The fire could go out. I might not be able to see it really well in time even if it is on and then you'll be downstairs with my things."

"They'll be there. The light will be good. That's the bargain we made. I won't go back on it. I'm no dope. I'm satisfied with just the tv set and getting away. Now let go of the ropes."

"Tod, Mary," I yell pounding on their door while still holding the ropes, "please get the flashlight from in front of your door and shine it down the shaft. You hear the burglar I'm talking to. I want to make absolutely sure he gives my money and watch back."

"Can't wait anymore." Cuts the ropes. I hear them sliding out of the pulleys or something above and then coming down and I let go of the rope I hold and duck in my apartment just before the rope falls past. It lands on the dumbwaiter roof. The man's smashing something. Wood. Kicks or beats out the floor of the dumbwaiter and jumps to the basement. "Yah, my leg. You crud. I should've stuck you in the head when I had the car on your floor." Match, blows it out. Limping, sounds from below. Door opening. I run to the front of the apartment, run back to the kitchen and get the knife and candlestick and run to the front of the apartment, hallway, flashlight's gone, down 3 flights and out of the building. A man's limping on the sidewalk about 50 feet away. I start after him when a police car pulls up in front of the building and a policeman in the righthand seat says "You, stop, drop what you have" and I see he has a gun pointed out the window at me.

"It's not me, it's him."

"Drop them count of 2 and raise your arms."

I drop the candlestick and knife and raise my arms. Candlestick rolls toward the gutter. "I'm Art Alimin, tenant 4W, apartment that was robbed just before. Burglar's just run out of our building basement from the dumbwaiter he had to break to escape and is now over there, getting away, going west. I still see him. Limping from his dumbwaiter fall. Carrying something it seems. Probably my tv. Maybe something else bulky he took I don't know about yet and the tv he left behind or broke in the fall. Now crossing the street. Looking back. Still limping. Just turned the corner."

Gun's withdrawn, back door opens, "Get in."

I start for the car, then back for the candlestick and knife.

"Leave them, get in."

Car starts up. "You," I yell out the back window to a woman passing. "Candlestick and knife, keep them for me please. We shouldn't be long. It's someone else's crime." She looks perplexed. "Candlestick's in the street." Waves and smiles she'll do it.

We drive around the neighborhood, sidestreets and avenues, more limping people than I ever noticed before, slowing up everytime we see one, woman or man, women only from the back. "He it?"

"No not the one," I say.

"Lady anyway. He could've gone anywhere. Subway, bus, cab, his own car, just melted away. Limp could've been a fake and set straight once he got around the corner, just to throw us off. Let's give up."

We drive back to the building. Woman's not there, candlestick and knife neither. We go to the basement. Every tenant has a key. Policeman inspects the door and says it wasn't broken in. Parts of the elevator car floor are in the basement, no trace of my tv, money, watch or his blood. Rope's cut so elevator car's stuck above the second floor.

"Quite a leap for no limp," I say.

"He could've known how to land and tv he probably hid in a dark place for another day in a nearby building areaway, that's why we didn't see him." He goes upstairs to speak to all the tenants. I talk to the other policeman in my bedroom while I pick the jewelry off the floor and put them in the box. Most of the new good stuff and all the heirlooms that I can remember seem to be gone. I write on the robbery report the items I think missing.

"Sure that's all?"

"Everything I can see."

"You haven't yet checked the rest of the drawers, the livingroom or hallway. He could've taken a good ashtray, a pillowcase of various things."

"The pillowcases seem to be there."

"You look in the linencloset?"

"I wouldn't know if one was missing. We have about 10 of them, all light blue. Some are in the hamper."

"Just look around your apartment and see what doesn't catch your eye. If you've insurance you'll get the value of what's missing back. Theoretically more if your things were listed new but bought imperfect and since deteriorated."

"We have no insurance except fire. I don't even have any for life."

"She have furs?"

"One. I never liked it. She did, was in love with it. An old leopard. She's not allowed to wear it anymore. Did around the house when it was freezing out and no heat in here and last Halloween at a party when she went as an alleycat. That time she wore a coat over the coat. Times before that people screamed at her on the street for killing leopards and tigers. One woman summoned a policeman and wanted her arrested. He had to call in to know what to do. A sergeant over the intercom had her swear never to wear it again or even admit to anyone she owns it and she wouldn't be brought in. The woman wasn't satisfied and sued in behalf of all endangered species. Suit's still pending. I even think Donna's to appear in court this week."

"See if it's missing."

I look. "Coat's not there."

"Put it down on the report if you're sure she didn't walk out with it on tonight. Maybe tonight's the one night she took a chance. Though it's too warm for even a longsleeve shirt for me and I wouldn't think so if she has to be at court this week because of the coat."

"Maybe you haven't heard, but this woman I live with, Donna Akers, has been missing for 3 days and all the police precincts are supposed to have alerts out for her."

"Akers, that's right. So she's your friend, lives here. Funny for only an hour ago we got radioed off that search because there was no sign of foulplay they said."

"What do you mean no foulplay? How do you expect to find out unless you look for her?"

"That's all I know. Troubles you, call our deskman if you want to know more."

I phone the station house. Deskman switches me to the commanding officer who says "Yes sir, it's right in the log here. You see, missing people can be tricky business. Our guidelines on it are everyone over 18 can disappear for as long as she or he likes so long as a routine investigation's been made to show there's no indication of foulplay. One was and there isn't. We found a few unusual things but concluded that Miss Akers left of her own freewill and probably impulsively or perhaps out of some form of benevolent coercion exerted over a prolonged period by someone unknown to us who she knew well enough to have refused had she wanted to without any fear of retaliation but out of no foulplay."

"How'd you reach that conclusion?"

"Through our investigation."

"What did you find?"

"What I told you."

"In less than several nighttime hours you investigated all the names and places I gave your detectives and possibly some in her diaries and letters I didn't know about and all the leads those names, places and writings might have produced?"

"All that were necessary to investigate. Remember the word routine."

"Which ones didn't you?"

"Why do you want to know?"

"So I can check them out myself."

"Those names I can't give you."

"Why?"

"Rights of privacy—hers and the names and places we investigated."

"What about the ones out of town?"

"You know if there were any?"

"She was in touch with people all over and worked all over too."

"Let me say that if there were any of these who had to be contacted, we did so by phone."

"Ones overseas too?"

"There are phones just about everywhere now—certainly wherever she might have traveled to or worked."

"She recently had a modeling assignment for umbrellas in a primitive rainforest in the other hemisphere with the local natives and their huts and dugs and dugouts as backdrops."

"It's surprising they went that far and were so extravagant in these abstemious times when you'd think they could get the same effect in one of our natural history museums."

"It was an expensive ad campaign because of the manufacturer's investment in the umbrella's bright new textile designs and revolutionary hinged ribs and portability, for it folded up to the size of a tablespoon. But my point's that the shooting crew were located several hours from the nearest phone."

"I'll concede we weren't aware of that area regarding Miss Akers, maybe because it didn't relate to her case."

"And your shortlived footwork here and phonecalls everywhere else—that sufficed to show there was no foulplay?"

"Many of our calls ended up in more calls and footwork by the police we made them to. But let me also say that if our work and these other officers' work hadn't been enough, we wouldn't have said our routine investigation was concluded."

"You went to the Coliseum?"

"Let me see? Yes and we found nothing. But I'm saying no more."

"I did too. Nothing. Though I haven't your adeptness at questioning. But did you know the cashier of the night we went to that theater was fired the next day or so? You speak to her?"

"What good would it do we decided. It's a big cheap movie house and she maybe sees a thousand customers a day. Short, bowlegged or bald: they're all blurs to her. Besides which she's just a petty thief caught in the act and penalized by losing her job when most everyone's crying for one and that's been her livelihood and delightful life almost always but no relationship to Miss Akers' disappearance."

"Then you admit she disappeared?"

"By the dictionary definition of the word, yes. Removed from sight. At least from the sight of everyone we think she knew who counted. Sure it's only been a few hours but take my word we've a big staff here that's gradually shrinking because of budgetary cuts but still large and thorough enough to get what we want done quickly and efficiently. And considering that today wasn't our busiest for lawbreaking and enforcement and fewer men reported in sick than usual or gave blood and got 2 days off, we concluded the investigation even more quickly."

"Did you know my apartment was burglarized tonight?"

"One has something to do with the other? Excuse me while I tell a caller to hold. —Go on."

"The 2 could. Burglar might've gotten in with her keys."

"That's your only access? I've got down here dumbwaiter, roof, fire escape."

"Only the front apartments have fire escapes. We're in back."

"Maybe that's what my men meant then. Through a front fire escape of some tenant's place to the public hallway and then into yours instead of trying to get in through the lobby door."

"My front door wasn't tampered with. It was doublelocked."

"How do you know you didn't leave it open when you left?"

"Because I never do, not even when I go downstairs for the mail. It's like a pot boiling. I know I might get distracted downstairs or go outside to get something and then the water will boil over or pot burn or just the flame go out and gas leak and somehow the kitchen set on fire or with my door open, a stranger could walk in, so I don't."

"What you think you never do and might suddenly in a rush without ever being aware you did it are 2 different things."

"That's what I'm saying in that with me I prevent that from the start by shutting off the gas burner and locking my door."

"So this time was the exception, not that I'm saying it was. But look. I've already put 3 callers on hold while I've been with you and now my fifth button is blinking which means my entire panel's tied up with emergency calls. Let me finally say this and hang up. Your being robbed and her disappearing are coincidental but not unusual. I can't reasonably see where the 2 connect unless the person in the dumbwaiter was her and she was playing an intricate joke on you that neither of us so far understand, which she of course didn't. But if you want I'll switch you back to the desk to report the theft, not that you'll have one chance in 50 of recovering any of your property or one in a 100 the thief will be found even if you have fingerprints with his face and address on them and he has a record with us an arm long."

"I've reported it. Police are with me now."

"You have? I don't see it on the log. Oh yeah, here it is. Apartment 2U. Under Alimin. I was looking for it under Akers and forgot. Put the cop in charge on if there's one."

Doorbell rings. "It's 4W," I say into the receiver and hand it to the policeman and answer the door. When the other policeman and I get back to the room, the policeman on the phone says to the one I let in "Lieutenant for you."

"No sir," he says on the phone, "Yes. Not the roof but could've ridden up on the dumbwaiter, but none of the other tenants were broken in.... Scared, everyone here, super included, of this Mr. Alimin, because they thought he was making up this man on the lift and they didn't know what else he'd do.... No, basement door was the kind that swings shut behind you automatically and locks itself and the super who said he was down there an hour ago swore it was locked secure.... Each apartment does have a key to it so somebody but the super could've but they all say they weren't.... No, he seems all right, quiet guy, nice wife and kids, supering and in this country for less than a year but good and honest tenants say and to me 2 feet too tall to fit in the dumbwaiter.... It's true, worked for the circus.... No sir, burglar couldn't have been in there already because the way the super said the door was locked was done with a key.... Turned, that's right and also snapped shut. Also ... Could've right after the super saw the door, true. Also, this same super has Mr. Alimin's extra set of housekeys and roof door was locked secure, so ... Bolted, so how the burglar got in the basement, if that was the place he came up from, less somebody left the basement door open soon after the super saw it, and the doorcheck for what the super says would be the first time since it was installed didn't automatically swing shut the door to lock, is a puzzle to us.... How he got in is ... Burglar ... Yes sir." Gives me the phone.

"Someone who's going to grab your girl off the street is not the same person to beat out with only a tv and measly dough and whatever jewels you had unless they're the crown heads of sovereign or something. One's kidnapping or murder, too much to risk getting caught going back for as you suggest the burglar did. He's the kidnapper, there would have been a ransom note by now. Why else unless he just wanted to sexually abuse her, though they don't usually do that for more than a day or 2 and she's been away 3. He's the murderer, they don't go back for any reasons but those crown jewels. They might be filthy, crazed, loathsome and often very stupid and worse, but when they kill someone they invariably charge up their smarts and sanity enough to stay away from the place they kidnapped her at and at least for a couple weeks keep test tube clean. That's my theory. I'll speak to the captain when he gets in in the morning. Meanwhile, give my boys everything they want to know. Have a good night."

"We haven't finished your report yet," one of them says. "Jewelry, money," sneezes. "Take the cat away please. Asthmatic." I put the cat in the bathroom. Opens the slightly ajar door with his nose and paw and I grab it, throw it back in and slam the door. Mewls.

"Shhh, really—I'll be back." Scratches and whines. "Dumb of me," I say to the men. "Donna's also allergic to cats and 33 other things that make her wheeze and sneeze and sometimes squint at death as she says and I forgot to tell the detectives that."

"Don't worry. She comes back, you can just throw it out."

"I mean if she suddenly needed her medicine—prescription antihistamine tablets and sprays, they'd have to send out for it. The pharmacies in the city could've been notified."

"You don't know them. They'd let her sneeze to death first. And no pharmacy wants to be firebombed for being the finger. Money, leopard, tv—"

"Don't list the coat. I don't even think she's supposed to have one at home. Someone said they all had to be turned in last year for no compensation along with anything alligator. Supposedly they can't even be used for a floor rug or wall hanging and if anyone sees and reports it, we can be brought to court, for we both signed the lease, and steeply fined."

"You said it missing, it has to stay in." They ask me to look for a number of other things we either don't have or aren't missing and then to sign the stolen items report so they can go.

"I'll sign it, but to me this is wasting precious time. He's the one, that burglar—has to be, how else? If he didn't grab her, had to at least find her purse or been given it or her address and keys to know where to and how to get in. So you should be on the street now trying to find him, and other patrol cars and men."

"We already determined he's gone."

"Only by car. What could we see out a window? Somebody might've spotted him on the street, going into a subway, carrying the tv or not, stopping at a crowded coffeeshop for a cup."

"He wouldn't do that. Once they go, and especially with a television, they get out of the neighborhood fast."

"He could live in the neighborhood. Somebody might've seen him entering his building. A newsdealer. I hear every street has its paid police spotter."

"Spotters stop spotting at 9, though you're not to know that, so don't say. And you've got a newsdealer open alone around here this hour, he's taking big chances if he is, even unalone."

"Doormen then. Locked behind it, safe, they can gaze through the glass. The burglar might've feinted left to make us think he was going that way and then crossed the avenue when he was out of our viewline and slipped up the next sidestreet from this heading west where there are several large apartment buildings with doormen. And a deli that's open till one."

"Doormen only look for tips. As for your deli guys, they're asking for it too if they're open now, and it's past one."

"He could be closing. One does. Dav, alone, has a doberman, right on this avenue corner the burglar ran up. I've seen him shutting his gates close to 2 sometimes. Says staying open late 7 days straight's the only way he can make money, holidays included. Let's go and check. Nothing to lose."

"We are hungry, so a deli's a good idea if you know one around here open where we can get some food. As for one seeing what you think's your man—"

"At least speak to him."

"If he's open, for a sandwich and beer. But you got to remember. There are plenty other apartments and cars getting knocked off around now which after our dinner break—"

I leave the room.

"Hey, where you think you're going?"

Out the apartment.

"Wait, you didn't sign. We don't want to have to come back. Listen, tranquilizer's what you need more and sleep. Sleep, Mr. Alimin, that's easy to see, but please sign this so we can also go."

Downstairs, street. Avenue, man locking the deli door, no dog. "Dav, hello, I have to talk to you—" jumps back, keys dropping, touches his heart: "God!"

"Sorry, thought you saw me." Pick up his keys. "But you see a limping man running past here before?"

"Running? I'm seeing stars you scared me so much. Last week—why you think there's no Fritz? 3 punks come in, shot him, clunked me on my head with their guns and stole and stole. They got so much, I thought you was them returned. Good thing I wasn't a dog: I'd be dead." Bends over to show me the red patch on his head. "Zipper's underneath: too big a ditch for thread."

"I'm really sorry."

"Why be: you're who to blame?"

"But this man, Dav. Maybe walking. Probably carrying my small tv set and maybe not limping. Possibly stopping at your store an hour, less than one ago or so. In my department—apartment—I don't know what he looked like or how he was dressed, but deep local voice possibly disguised. Also a leopard coat. Not on but over his arm most likely, for it's gone too."

"I didn't. But a leopard's what I could use, forget your coat. Or a lion. But I'm getting 2 big Danes trained now, for the back and front and to walk me home. Just feeding them will cut my profits 10 percent and customer and living space 25. Because big as their mouths are and born killers, dobermans don't scare the punks away anymore, though only having Fritz here yawning used to give me the creeps."

"What about Donna lately? See her around?"

"Who's her?"

"Woman I live with. Came in here with me a few times and also alone. Tall, inch more than me, 3 to 4 with platforms or heels. Slim. Always kidding with you guys. Model. In fact her photo's one of the ones up on your store wall above the board you make the sandwiches on."

"She her? Goodlooker. I didn't put you 2 together, though I'm sure you have. Picture was there one day when I come in. Must've given it to my dayman, Ray. Tacked it up crumpled because I think he had it under his mattress first. I've seen her, not yesterday or today. Week ago last. Potato salad. Watch my memory: pound of it southern style and smoked ham and half pound of cole slaw. Ham sliced thin. I remember saying 'Thin as you are I can never get it sliced.' She laughed. I'm sure to be polite. Because I later thought to myself what a dumb joke I made. Gross. An insult. Thin to her might be an affliction. I even slapped my head in disgust, something I wouldn't do since the attack. And pickled tomatoes she asked for too. 'A tomato you'll be till you're 80,' I told her, 'but pickled I don't ever think so, you're too sweet and nice.' She laughed again and said 'You never know.' But stupid ungracious incurable dumb insults I always make. What's with me I later thought and always forever. I can't control myself. Women customers ask me for big dills and my mouth goes out of my head. Sex on my mind all the time and dirty old deliman kind, not healthy like a lady like she should bring out in me. But her? Go home. Forget your limping man. She'll be waiting with her new lingerie off for you, but it's no good to get innocent people like me involved for her to later get mad at for sticking our big noses in. For sticking something else in, that's altogether different where we wouldn't so much mind, no offense. Because whatever it is between you 2, what could I do to help and why should I feel so sorry for you? One hour alone with her any way I liked I'd give up 10 pounds of potato salad for, northern or southern style, and a whole smoked ham. But I don't interfere noways in domestic strifes, policy rule." Pulls the gate across the storefront, padlocks. "Walking my way?"

"Maybe the doorman in number 70 saw him."

"Maybe but why?"

"Maybe you didn't hear me before: I got robbed tonight."

"No, that didn't come across clear. You saying by 3 young punks with gun butts, clunked on the head, underground gouge?"

"My apartment by a burglar I only saw from afar. Came up that street. A limping man, bad left leg, probably carrying a small tv set and leopard coat."

"That's the one? I thought he was the man your sleek beauty run away with for the night while you was watching a tv show on zoos. You have to excuse me. I'm not so well with the head one week after my brains get mashed in. Doctor said I should vacation for a month, which I'd do if I had his business or he took over my 12 hour shifts those days. No, I didn't see him or she and even if I did see, what do I need now next, my store window smashed out which I can't even get insured no more? Tight lips, that's my best insurance, and when they run at me in the streets with blades, to pretend I'm a penniless crazy. Aiee—get the spittle to spout out of my mouth. Meanwhile I got to get home and hope my wife and apartment haven't been broken in too. Old people, you might know, have become the latest main targets."

"I'm sorry."

"Save your sorries. You'll be old too soon enough and I wouldn't want to be alive then. As for when your children become golden adults—don't have them."

I go to number 70. No other pedestrians around. Few cars. Empty buses. All the stores, bars, cafes are closed. Siren's still going. Train sounds from along the river. Night flyway, so procession of planes overhead. Apartment windows facing the street are dark. I knock. Doorman's sitting on a stool at the end of the long lobby, reading a book. Looks up, studies me, comes to the door. "What?"

"Very simple and quick. You see a limping man pass here about an hour ago? Maybe carrying—"

"Can't understand you. Too late for tonight." Book behind ear, raised brows, points to watch, shakes head and finger no, says get away with a hand wave, turns to go.

"Please, it's very important. Open the door if you can't hear me, but I think I'm speaking loud enough."

"Now yes, too loud. You wake tenants. Only open for people who live here or previous told about guests—building bylaw. This is a co-op, so what owners want. Owners tenants. Your name is what, I look on my list, though I know you not one as I met all their names before." Takes list out of hat and reads it. "You Saveen? No. You Macadoy? No. You—"

"I live on the next block. I'm looking for a man who burglarized my apartment tonight and perhaps kidnapped my best friend off the street 3 days ago. So one or the other reasons or both, I want to find him."

"See? You no one. I been fooled once too many to opening this door for young girl and then jumped on by 2 men, tied up. Beaten. Right thumb paralyzed for life and steal me and 30 apartments by time morning rose. No sirree no. Think I some dunce? Tenants pay well and give me one last time not to blow it and I don't."

"Just tell me yes or no if you saw him. It's quite simple. You did, I'll go further up the block to the next avenue and ask anyone there who might've been around then if they saw him. Doormen. Like those. That way, who knows? Maybe, possibly, farfetched, lunging at straws, sure, but I still might be able to track him down. Nobody's seen him around. I'll go home, but I at least tried. Watch. He was probably walking the way I'll do now. And carrying a small tv and leopard coat." I limp past the door. He stares, hand on his chin. I walk my natural way to the spot I started limping from and limp past the door again.

"Hey wait, I get my camera."

"Just answer yes or no."

"Yes, get moving. No?—I call the cops."

I jiggle the door handle. "A straight answer. You see him?"

"Hey, none of that. I give you straight—special direct straight line to police station and not afraid to use it. You want? I do." Presses a tile in the wall and small door springs open. Pulls out a one-button phone from inside the hole and shows it to me.

I go to the curb. He puts the phone back and returns to the stool. Cab pulls up, man steps out, sees me, says to the driver "Wait till I get inside."

"Sure, for another quarter. Meter's off."

"That's the spirit." Gives him a coin and rings building bell. Doorman looks up. Angry till he sees it's not me but someone he knows. Smiles. Comes to the door and opens it. Cab drives off. "You—don't make me madder, get," he tells me. "Goodnight, Mr. Chantz, have a nice evening?"

"Very pleasant, Dester. You?"

I go. One of the 3 other doorman on the block comes to the door and says through it after I ask: "No limper, no tv, no carrier, no coat."

"Thanks." I head home.

"Say pal, take a moment?"

I jump. Man stepping out of a store doorway. I'm about to bolt.

"Don't panic. I'm far from harm." Sleeves torn off his white dress shirt, one shoe on, no socks, holding up his pants, young.

"I'm in a hurry, sorry."

"I know, me too. Hurry hurry, what's to worry? So spare a half dollar or subway token? Lost all mine through a pants pocket rip and have to get home. 4 roughs slugged me when I left a bar."

"Come on, I've seen you."

"When, where?"

"2 nights ago to be exact. Lots of other nights and days, for months. Mostly around the park asking for change. I once even gave you."

"Never me."

"Then I gave to myself, maybe twice. 'Spare some change?' I asked and in another voice said 'Sure' and handed my other hand a dime. You always wear the same clothes or different but torn up—I remember the no sleeves."

"That must be my younger brother Bernard. Mine were always nice till tonight—workmen's but clean. I'm uptown and have to be by subway there where my sister is who I live with."

"I'm sorry but I know it was you. See ya."

"What are you? Wait. Tell me. You're no cop?"

"Yes. No, I'm lying, I'm not."

"Well all right then, all right. Put it there." We shake. "Now got a half dollar to loan?"

"I'm also broke."

"Okay, that's all you had to tell me. That's what's the trouble with the world—too much to say." Goes back into the doorway.

"One more thing if you don't mind. You've been standing here long?"

"You know all about what I do so you tell me. Though I will admit I saw you whisk past this way before but you were too in a mood to be stopped."

"See a limping man come the same way an hour ago more or less?"

"Limping?" Steps out. "With his leg?"

"Yes."

"Plenty. What color?"

"I didn't see him."

"Age, size then. Not plenty but several as they were all the colors and each around the same age but assorted sizes. Short, medium, fat, others, more."

"I never saw him. But judging from his voice, around my age. 40 to 50 and probably carrying a small tv and leopard coat, for those are what he stole from our place."

"Caught the small tv but no coat. Wasn't wearing one. A shirt. Pants. Shoes. Want more, well I really could use a half dollar to get home. That was no crap. Or say a dime to call my sis. She's got a young son, no husband, bad neighborhood and gets worried for her only kin left except her kid. The brother, years of sponging off us, we both disowned."

"I'll get it from my apartment. A dollar even. I'm on the next block."

"Forget it. I walk there with you, you'll get me up some way. Who knows what you'll do. Notice my swollen cheek? This scab, that hole? I can show you the scars and newest marks all over my back and butt and in it and on my thighs, when they came at me in 3's and 4's. Pigs in this pot." Spits, steps back till I can't see him. Feet. No feet. A nose. Fingertip. Flicks what he picks, then no part of him, dark doorway.

"I'll bring it down then. Stay here."

"You'll bring down a gun or bat to shoot me or whatever you want by force. That could be a fact, so no thank you, sport. Though you're really serious, what you got to give on you now?"

"Relatively nothing." I search my pockets. Keys. Fountain pen. Folded old hanky. I hold the pen out to him.

"No thanks. But I will tell you your friend wasn't carrying the tv like it was his own. Not like it was a baby so careful with it like you and I'd be. If it fell he'd even be relieved it seemed. Good: have no more one mouth to feed—got it?"

"He could be the one. What he look like? Color, hair, clothes, build?"

"Pull all your pockets out." I do. "Turn so I can see. Watch pocket?"

"Forgot." Find a penny in it. "You don't want this."

"Lucky penny—you bet." Steps out. "Maybe everything will change for the better now. Give it." Do. "Maybe for you too." Rubs it. "Blow."

"Come on."

"Blow on it, make a wish." I blow on it. "Make a wish." Close my eyes and think what could I wish about. I can't wish about anything. I'm not a wisher. What am I doing here? Do I believe this man? Why should I? I've reason. He hasn't been shown wrong yet. Says he knows. He might know. "Wish. You're not." Move my lips saying nothing while I wish that Donna would walk along this street, yell my name and run to me, arms out, arms in, whatever, even with a loving man in tow, his hand in hers, I wouldn't care, but just to be there, though hopefully to throw her arms around mine and say "I'm here, love, where you been? Just a bit of capriciousness, but now I'm home." I open my eyes. His are closed. "Star bright, star light, or star light, star bright, first penny of the night. I wish for more, I pray for thousands. A fortune, not just a token. Taxis, limousines. Fine wines and dining and girls and best possible of worlds and hot towels, fancy shoes, marvels, revels, the best of the cream of the rest and my nephew a private school." Drops penny in his pocket. "Shirt pocket?"

"Have none. That's it."

"Shoes then. Shake them upside down."

"If they weren't loafers, I doubt I would." I slip them off and shake them. Pebble drops out. Hadn't felt it.

"Okay. A coat. Couldn't see what exact color in the dark except for the black spots. Leopards have spots. So I'll settle it's a leopard when I didn't think anything what it was then. No cause to. Coat's a coat to me, even when over the arm and heavy on a summer day."

"What about his looks? Clothes. Built big or small and his hair."

"What else is in it for me?"

"What could it be? My belt? It's good leather. Bought it through a mail order house up north and guaranteed to last for life. Doesn't, just send it back to them, address is stenciled on the belt's inside, and without questions or the original bill they'll send you a new one of even a different size that'll also be guaranteed for life and pay the postage both ways, reimbursing you by check for your parcel post costs. You haven't one on. If it's too large, punch in another hole." I pull it off, hold my pants up while I hold the belt out to him.

"Your friend looked like this," putting the belt on. "Hey I'm free, my hands are free, I can now if I want really run fast," laughs. "Average height for today. Same skin color as yours from what I can see at night. Maybe an inch taller or shorter or shade darker or light. Fits perfect. What are you, a 32 too? Full face, unmarked, fish lips, all like you. Wide eyes, I don't know how dark. Normal head of hair. Long gray sideburns like you, dark on top, thinning temples not that far back. Ears which didn't stick out that much. Not the largest nose. Remember, this is all kind of a quick observation but a sharp one, right? considering I didn't suppose him of anything then so had no reason to observe him close. Thick neck with a lump in his throat that stuck way out. You have no lump or you're hiding it or it only comes out special times that you can't control. Believe me he looked like you if you limped. If you also had a spotted coat and tv, I wouldn't know you from him. Far as I saw, dressed the same too. Belt I'm sure, though you differ that way unless he's thrown his away now so as not to be recognized. He went up the sidestreet you just came down, also in a hurry. Why the worry? I asked him for a half like I did you. He said to get lost. Fair enough. Foreign voice. I couldn't tell where from."

"Man I'm interested in didn't have a foreign voice."

"Maybe his also didn't. I'm from a foreign country. You know—originally, so to me maybe though I speak like a native now, I might still not hear like one and so the native could still sound foreign to me. You a foreigner?"

"No a native."

"You sound like a native, so I could be wrong or right, depending if my hearing theory's correct. And small portable tv."

"What kind?"

"Professionally made. Pretty new. 10 to 16 inch tube in a woodenlike cabinet. I don't know makes. But screen, knobs, I think antenna tucked in on top."

"Mine had no antenna."

"This one I thought might have, but with shadows and night and all, who could really tell? I did ask him what program he's watching. Sometimes I think I'm funny. He didn't, but I can also say for sure he didn't have the sense of respect you seem to. And his big rush, almost running. You could say he was running for a limper. I kept up with him for seconds but couldn't for longer because I had no belt. Now I could, not that I'd want to, as all I wanted was a coin from him, not to win a race."

"Remember which leg he was limping on?"

"Maybe both. He just limped, up down, up down, and went up that sidestreet. That's where my eyes stopped following him, rest of my body long before. I went back to this door. Hour ago like you said. It's taken me that long now to get just one 50th of my fare home. I keep along that ratio, I'll be 2 whole days here before I get it all."

"Thanks and take the pen. It uses real ink. Cost me 5 bills once. The new ones, same brand and make, now go for 7.50, though the boxes they come in still say 5."

"That's different. I thought it was just cheap imitation ballpoint, made to soil my hands." Takes it. "Should get 49 cents for it at least if anyone else interested in good pens is on the streets. I'm sure if I stopped you without knowing you and you had 49 cents, you'd give that much for it if it wasn't your last change."

"Even if it was and I knew you, it'd be a bargain."

"Well come around then and give me 49 cents for it and I'll give you your pen back. You have just a half dollar piece, I got change."

I go up the sidestreet. Walk slow because I have to hold up my pants. I've lost a lot of weight lately it seemed. Maybe in the last 3 days, or else my pants always fit like this without a belt. Nobody's around. Everything's closed. Go down the subway station and woman in the token booth says "No, I didn't see anyone with a tv or leather coat." I describe the man the way the panhandler said he looked and she says "I didn't see anyone like that either, limping or normal walk. But they fly by so quick and all seem like hands with change or green in them other than when they stick me up or run through free, so don't trust so fast with what I swear I didn't see. I can say positively he didn't rob me."

Upstairs, planes still overhead. No buses or cabs on the street and very few cars. I head home.

"Say pal, take a moment?"

"You got me tonight."

"That's right, didn't see there from the dark who it was. Find your friend?"

"No. By the way, if there's anything I have to ask you later on from what I forgot to before, you have a name and phone number or address? Anything. A flophouse where they know you if that's all there is, for it's important enough where I'll try."

"Dial erratic."

"Kidding me again?"

"When did I do before? Dial it. E-r-r- and the rest of the way they spell it and you'll get me, my nephew or sis. Kid can hear and write okay but only speaks sign language, but sis's got her m.a. And you still have no change?"

"Right."

"Because I have this nice pen and belt. Okay. Goodnight."

Home, phone. "You bastard," Louis says. "You should know by now not to give my names out for anything anytime to cops. I'm in bad trouble now, bastard. They look one look at me when they be here and right away say where's my green card? They say nothing or ever even come here if I never sleep with your dumb broad and so know you through her."

"All I did was mention you as one of her friends. I'm sorry."

"That's just it. You supposed to say nothing, mention no one. How long you live here? Me I live here one year and know that in weeks. My green card I have none. I lost it. That's the truth, that's I tell them. They call immigration people right from where I'm standing now to you on phone and immigration say they be right over right away. I'm leaving now. Baggage, that's all. They find me they send me home, so they never find me because they never let me come back. I give up good room for good that took me long time to find because of you and good furniture too. You bastard. If I find you I want to kill you but think I won't. Just to do it I'll be in worse trouble now they know I know you. I wish I never screwed your Donna or met her. She bad lay. She worse news. Big legs, so what?—she's no brains or tits, probably like you. You lucky you alive, bastard, and deserve her the most. In my country fools like you do that they have their ears sliced off. Do it twice, out goes their hearts with a special curve knife."

"What country's that?"

"None your business, don't be wise."

"I meant I was curious even from the first time I phoned you. I've never quite heard an accent like yours, not that I'm criticizing it."

"I said watch out, don't be smart. This is real truth from the heart last time to you, bastard. Once I worry hard about you both but now no more. Now wish you dead forever, you and your damn Don."

I bite the rest of my nails down past their white marks and apply iodine to them, sweep up and throw out the mess from the hairblower I broke in the bathtub, try and hammer out Donna's ancestral candlestick I dented when I first searched for the burglar, oldest thing she owns, clean up and pour ammonia on the floor where the cat made, go to bed. Siren alarm. Phone.

"You the fella who yelled for Donna Akers from a roof before?"

"Yes," turning on the light. "Know where she is?"

Note near the phone: Man   out.   Wont   me. Police

"Are you sleepy? You sound sleepy."

I blink my eyes and rub them with my fingers. "I am but I—"

"Because I can call back now that I know where to."

Man called when your out. Wont leave name. Said hell call again. Police

"No, tell me what it is." Another note on the floor, pick it up.

Woman named Joe Anne called too. Said nothing new. Anything with you? (she said.) Your to call her. Police

"Are you sure? It's no trouble to call back. Later today, next if you want. If you have something better to do or to sleep, do so, but I don't want to feel I must wheedle you into hearing me."

"You don't. I'm up and this is too important. What about her? Though you the one who called before and another man answered?"

"Are you going to let me speak or not? Anyway, no, I heard you on your roof. I thought I said that. First I thought: holy, what noise. But then I knew I could help you. I got her name from the book. Akers D. I didn't know yours since you didn't say, but you did tell a dog man you were arguing with on the roof that she was your friend there, so I put together 2 plus 2. I'm an old goat myself and you can't know how tough a name like hers is to look up."

"Just tell me: you know where Donna is?"

"Shut up. From now on, don't interrupt. There's already been too many delays with you. If you do, I leave and now won't come back. Where was I? You can't know how tough a name like hers is to look up. I looked up Akers like aches her from pain and then lots of people who ache like plural 2 or more. And Akers like the land amount plowed by a yoke of oxen in one day once. And next the same land amount as I used to think it was spelt when I was a boy, with an a-c-e-r-s, which I still think is how it should be written today. And even the Akers like the maple tree, but none of these were at the approximate address across the street where I thought you and she lived, numbers 1 through 19 East. Shrubs and leaves being my true hobby, you'd think I would have thought about the maple Akers first, since it's such a common genus hereabouts. Till I tried the one Akers I felt left unless you can come up with another and saw the letter D and knew it was her, though in the end it was you I was actually looking for."

"That's very kind of you. But looking for me for what?"

"Not kind—please. As you said before, it's very important, so naturally that's why I called. But you will let me finish now that you've let me start, won't you?"

"Go ahead. You saw her or know something about her?"

"I said you will let me finish without further interventions, now on that are we agreed?"

"If I say anything, even this, or that yes I agree, you might accuse me again of interrupting or not letting you finish. I don't know what to say. I want you to finish. But I'm eager to know about her which is why I constantly interrupt you and I think I'm also much sleepier than I thought. But I want to hear what you have to say. I do. So don't let anything I say stop you. Please go on. Excuse me."

"This is the last time I'm warning you, do you understand that?"

I don't speak. 30 seconds, minute. Nothing's said by either of us.

"Fine. Because if you had said one word more, a breath even that sounded like a word or the reverse, I would have hung up. Now do you want to know where Miss Akers is? though don't answer that. I'll know by your silence. If you say anything, it will mean you don't want to know and by now you know what that will mean."

30 seconds, minute.

"You haven't hung up yet, have you? If you had, I would have heard some sort of hanging up noise."

Minute, 2.

"Then you want to know. Fine. I saw her leave by telescope tonight. Not by telescope but through it. I saw her. She's far away by now, miles, and that's not just a guess. She set forth from the front of your apartment house with an odd looking one-eyed chap with seemingly only a single long leg running down from his crotch like a stork's, though I'm sure that was only an illusion like the stork's because his legs were so close together and so thin and because he had on such narrow dark trousers and tapered dark shoes. That's what I saw through my window telescope when I accidentally moved the tube down from up. Though I still have more to say, so for your own sake don't say anything till I say it's all right to, agreed?"

Minute.

"Fine. I know this is unusual and that I'm even being a little unfair to you. But this is the way I want it—not for anyone for a few minutes to interrupt me. The reason is I'm retired and old. That's not why I want it though it might be because of it. People don't listen to me, maybe because they think I am retired and old and thus having nothing to say or that I'll say too much. Or when they do listen it's only for a few seconds out of respect and then they interrupt and from then on dislike being interrupted by me, which I can well understand: people don't like being interrupted at any age. But you know I have something to say so you'll continue to listen. And everything I'm telling you about her and myself is the truth—that you must believe for your own sake. Incidentally, I wanted to say your given name at the end of the word sake. What is it?"

Seconds.

"It's all right. I won't consider that interrupting, though just to say your name."

"What's yours?"

"Don't try me again. What's mine is my name but yours is what? Because I'm the one who hasn't finished giving what I'm certain you'll find to be the most informational data about Miss Akers yet."

"Art."

"Then you do believe everything I'm telling you about her and myself is the truth, Art, yes? —Fine. Where was I? Telescope and man with legs like a thin stork's or thin man's thin legs looking like a stork's, but you know. And he was quite thin. Though he could walk fast enough if it was only one leg he had or the 2 were stuck. But I'm sure it only looked like that because of the way the light was behind me—some fluke in reflection or perspective or my own defective sight. My telescope also isn't the greatest. And I'm still, incidentally, following their movements. If you'd like to watch them with me, my name's Lepage, in number 20 across the street, bell without the nameplate under it—people who I don't like I don't like to be disturbed by, and I also have an unlisted phone number, so what do you say?—You wouldn't like? —Then if you'd prefer, watch them with me in just a verbal way. My eye on the eyepiece, telescope cocked tight, there they are again, the 2 of them, still holding hands kissing cute, quarter ways by now to the moon I presume and I bet in a week or less a bit beyond it to the universe behind, or vice versa, though don't deduce I know as much about astronomy or uranography as I do about trees and shrubs."

"Excuse me, but do you know how you've affected me? My worry's real, Donna's my whatever she is to me, and I believed you at first."

"Shut up. Don't talk. If you do, I'll hang up."

"Your calling and contriving this tale because you happened to hear me screaming outside—"

"Don't tell me. You're all lies anyhow." Hangs up.

Calls back a minute later. My light's out, I'm in the beginning of dreaming. "The truth is, Art, I don't know where she's gone, or even if she is gone, though the latter's a matter you might like to kick around another time. I want to be your friend nevertheless. That's the truth too. You were extremely nice to me. My name isn't Lepage and I'm not old and retired—far from it. Nor do I live in number 20 of this or any street in this city or in any city or habitational place. I do have a bell without a name under it and a mediocre telescope. Those elaborated on lies before were simply to see if I was speaking to Miss Akers' friend. I'm still not positive I am speaking to him so I'll stop now, say goodnight, and please forget what I told you in the last call was the truth except for the nameless nameplate and telescope."

Phone rings a few minutes later. "Yuh."

"Everything I said in my last call—"

"I'm sleeping will you?"

"Let me say this and that will be all. Everything I said in my last call is not true. Neither the nameless nameplate nor mediocre telescope or anything else I mentioned such as I don't know where she has gone or even if she is gone or that I want to be your friend. I don't. You haven't been extremely nice to me or any other wise. I think she is gone and I just might know where she is. I might even live across the street and have a nameplate with my name on it, though you won't ever know what the address is or my name."

"You heard me from the roof so I know you live nearby, not that I'm interested anymore."

"I was visiting someone."

"Then you know someone who lives nearby, but leave me alone."

"What if I wasn't visiting anyone but in your neighborhood for something else?"

"I don't care. I don't want to speak to you. I want to sleep but also to leave my phone on the hook to receive any possible calls from Donna or about her that might be real. You know that so don't call."

"I was delivering a package to a person who happens to live near you, that's true. Whether a man or woman I won't say, but not someone I know, so it wasn't exactly a visit but a delivery. I was getting paid. Or someone could have called to tell me what you yelled from the roof and given me your general address—that could also be true."

"You live nearby. So what. I'm not getting after you. Now goodnight." I hang up.

Calls right back. "Yes, but not across the street. Forget I called."

"Okay."

"Say anything else, Art, and I won't go on. I'll hang up for good."

"Look, it's not I don't sympathize with your situation, but never call again."

"I warned you." Hangs up.

Gabe? Too late to phone him. If he's in, he'd be asleep. Not in, what can I do for him right now? In the morning then. I turn out the light. Cat jumps on the bed and scratches me through the sheet. I push it off the bed. Jumps back on and scratches me through the sheet. Light on, I slap its paw. Backs off but stays on the bed, waving its slapped paw at me. "What is it? You hungry? Or just obnoxious? Well I'm sleepy." Still shaking its paw. I go into the kitchen, cat walking beside me. All out of eggs, I mix bread crumbs and water in a bowl and put it on the floor and go to bed and turn off the light. Cat jumps on the bed and lies on my feet and seems to scratch and lick itself all night.

Phone rings when I'm asleep. Rings many times, different times, before I'm able to answer it. "One more thing you should know, Art, and that's—" I hang up. Calls right back. "One more thing and that's it, I swear. My name was once Lepage or let's just say it was the family name of someone in my family once, though who and how far back that goes and what section of this country or the country that person might have emigrated from if that was when this distant or close relative had the name Lepage, I won't say. But are you still interested in locating Miss Akers?"

"Just to sleep. Swear too. Thanks." Hang up.

Several more times during the night or in my sleep or both but I'm unable to answer it. One time, in or out of a dream, I get my hand on the receiver, when the ringing stops.

I wake around 11 and call Beverly.

"Hi, this is Bev on her answering machine. No it's not. Hello?"

"Hello, Beverly, it's Art. I want to—"

"Yes it is. Sorry about that. I won't erase it either. The urge to play games with these machines is overpowering, isn't it, though I suspect when almost everyone has one that fun will stop. Anyway, I was suddenly called out of town on business again. Life of the busy bee. If I tell you for how long—well, my new friend, I won't say his name, though I know one of you knows it, for you introduced us, cautioned me never to say on the machine that I'll be in tomorrow midday, as I did yesterday. Or that I'll be away for a week or a month or so on, for that way a stranger who might feel my flat's ripe for ravaging and call to see if anyone's home, could then slip in knowing he'll be unobstructed and alone. But, criminal stranger, news is my flat isn't ripe anymore and has in fact been overraped. I'm near to being destitute and part of the credit goes to the likes of you. All my sugar's on me including my passbooks and costume jewels and whatever there was of value here has been pinched or shat upon or rended or burned in 3 previous burglaries this calendar year. So what I hope I'm thwarting most in unfolding all this are the repair costs for my door locks being picked or door being kicked down and cleaning up the fruitless mess you'll make, unless you're solely after my underwear, skirts and hose. If you are, don't break in. Be cool. Simply tell me your measurements and pet colors and p.o. box number, honey, and I'll mail you some of these garments. If we're not the same size or I don't have your colors, I'll buy and have them sent to you, since that will mean a lot less cleaning up for me and moneywise I might even come out ahead on the deal. Anyway, since these business trips usually last a half day to a week or more, and I'm not saying what hour and date I recorded this message or how much luggage I took with me if any at all, decide for yourself friend, acquaintance, workperson, parent, latent or arrant potential burglar or sexual misfit, how long I'll be gone. But don't phone my office as no one there will give you any more info than I have, unless you say the magical mystical male name which isn't Shelly, Sid or Babe. So now, at the sign of the beep—oops, almost forgot you Art. No, we haven't seen hide or hair of her since Tuesday late and I've consulted the whole crew. I know she's booked for a shampoo shoot with Rom Betelvine for the next 2 days and then for some knitted cap snaps after that. I'll get back to you soon and I know Rom will be fuming to us too if she's not there by noon, but it has to be all right, yes? I tried calling you earlier but nobody answered and this trip suddenly materialized and I need all the beans I can bake to buy things for my burglars to take or they'll get so frustrated at always finding naught that they'll destroy my lovely place and the rest of my clothes. Now back to whoever wants to leave a message, since I didn't mean to turn these instructions into a ponderous discourse. Bye. Have a great day. And I'm truly sorry, Art, and feel helpless. As for everyone else who knows model Donna A, call Art Alimin at 324-1279, that's 324-1279, if you have any information, suspicions or clues where she could be, but don't get unsettled as I'm certain it'll work out okay. Peace." Beep.

"Bev, Art. No more false starts?—Good. I must've been asleep. Donna's still gone. Police won't help. I'll check Betelvine but let me know where Donna might have been or worked Wednesday till now. Any recent men friends of hers other than Louis Telegrin and Thomas Memblaise you might know of, even one-night stands or would-bes, don't spare me. I'm sick over it. Really. Sick. Diaries of hers the police read to me talked of an ex-husband and a child she gave up for adoption years ago, besides our lousy sex. Was I such an unsupportive or self-concerned emotional blank that she couldn't tell me or do you think she was exaggerating? Right now it's 11 Monday morning. Also, sorry to bother you so much about it and my feelings. No I'm not. Monday the 12th, just in case you're away for more than a week, because what could be more important if she's in danger or some predicament? Even that she owes money, whatever, I don't know, though I'm beginning to think anything's possible, or I hope. And hell with the police. No offense to them but we'll find her ourselves. What I plan to do, and if I could get a couple friends to help me that'd be great, and I'm sure I shouldn't have mentioned her diaries to you, is to go—" Beep. Dial tone.

I call back. "Hi, this is Bev on her answering machine. No it's—" I don't want to listen again or feel I've the time to and hang up.

I call Gabe. Not in. Call again and then Joanne at work: "Nothing, right? What do you think, Art, and truth now."

"When didn't I give it?"

"Then just tell me."

"What do you know?"

"I don't know if I still think she's missing. She might be and then again maybe not. In other words, I'm less sure than before and don't know anything more about it than I told you already, but that's what I think: we might be getting upset over nothing."

"I still think she's missing."

"Of course she's missing. But what I mean by missing is missing without anything bad happening to her or that she didn't bring on herself. I don't even know if I mean that—the last thing I said."

"What could she have brought on herself?"

"That's what I said—I don't know if I mean she did. Because she didn't drink, right? Not a secret one—no, just a wine drop here, half tonic and vodka squirt there—that was her limit, never beer, except maybe at parties when if she got a little high it was on 2 weak drinks she always regretted the next day and swore off of forever for a month. And did she play the tables or cards for big stakes? You bet. 2 half dollar lottery tickets every month from a candystore and that was her limit there. She even won once—a thousand, I couldn't believe it, wouldn't. Other than for maybe this disappearance thing, she was the luckiest sonofabitch I know. We each bought 2 half dollar tickets from the same lady that day, she first. Her second ticket won so I was one away from winning the money myself. I could have killed her. Not seriously. I mean if Donna does turn up dead, god forbid, and they ask you about anything I said—no, perish that, too hideous. She'll soon show up chipper and in the prime of health, but what else?"

"Else about what?"

"Bringing things on yourself. Men. Okay, we know she knew plenty, but none killers or kidnappers, correct? Maybe all into the masculine trip a bit except maybe you—but you, I'll tell the truth, I don't know so well after what, 3 years? and some more truth to your ears is Donna said she never knew you that much too. But I never saw one of these other men or heard from her where they acted with anything but sweet or deep feelings for her and incredible generosity, not like my Mark. Sure, she was tall and exceptionally gorgeous and men flashed on her all the time, but beauty doesn't count. It counts a lot in this world but not in the woman being accountable as if she brought it on herself for men being drawn to you, or to her, for as beauties go, we both know I'm not, while that girl was blessed. But what's left?"

"This fellow Telegrin was sort of a lawless and short-tempered character I thought. Talking with him, I was surprised she knew him so well and couldn't see him showing her much respect, not that I think he's involved in her being missing."

"Louis? She had him around her forefinger. Louie get this, if she wanted, Louie that. It was a public joke. He was 6-4 and built like a gymnast and very witty and articulate in his own country besides being rich and prominent there he said, but with her he mostly whimpered around like the skimpiest puppy. But we're all a little lawless, Art—admit it, even you."

"I don't know what I do that's so lawless."

"That leopard coat."

"Donna's."

"Your income taxes then. You don't cheat a little and wouldn't a lot?"

"No in both. Taxes have to be gathered and I could get caught if I didn't pay. And I feel better and safer when I play it straight and what the hell, if we want those laws changed like any laws then let's legally change them."

"Oh don't think you're so pure. I'll tell you something else, if you still don't mind hearing—if anything, your purity's what turned Donna off about you the most. She was dying for you to get crazy angry at her over nothing one day or to really do someone or some institution in criminally for a change, rather than the reverse. Your high moral tone drove her nauseous she said. Sometimes. Usually she said the nicest things about you and I'm certain she really loved you deep down. But drugs. That's what's left out of the bad things I thought she could have brought on herself and what I was driving at before. She—yes sir, it's a business call. —For Mr. Morini, who else? —Sorry, I didn't intend it that way and he's out on his rounds for an hour, this is research. —The librarian I'm speaking to doesn't know 2 times 2 and I'm not afraid for her to hear me say that to you, which is what's making this call so long. —Yes sir, and you too, nice day, thanks. —That fart. I have to go Art, he's still watching. Screw you, I hate your guts. I'm saying that to him—my boss's boss and public enemy number one around here, with the eyes and ears and smell too I'll tell you of a hawk. Ring me back in 5 and if someone answers but a woman, say pardon me you got the wrong number and hang up."

I feed the cat, clean up its mess, fill its box with fresh paper and grab its neck and squat its body in it and say "Here, this is where you're to make, not on the couch, table or floor." Phone rings. "Jo?"

"Mr. Alimin? I heard Beverly Windograde talk about Donna A on her message phone just now and want to ask whether it's still true."

"You know Donna?"

"Not really I believe. But it sounds terrible and I want to know if she's really gone, plain as that, poof, vanished, never came back?"

"Yes, but I don't see what it means to you, at least not so far."

"How long ago?"

"Just tell me why you want to know."

"What does Donna look like if I can ask?"

"How do you know Bev?"

"We're old friends. I was her client. Model. Quite big once. Lem Katlog. Mostly cigarettes and those little cigars they also wanted women to smoke. Now I sell shoes. It isn't easy. Got banged on the head by a brick one night walking in my very nice neighborhood then and lost part of my senses, an eye, most of my looks and have this big empty space of hair on my head too. And an ear was bruised some of it away too. Now I sell shoes. Children's. This brick didn't walk up and leap at me and bang my head if that's what I made it come out like. Nor was I crawling on the ground when it did. And there was victim's compensation but not much. Yet even yet, Bev and I keep in touch. We'll always be close, even if I don't make money for her anymore. She's good that way. But it's true? Because if it is about Donna, it's amazing."

"What is and why?"

"What is and why? My first wife. If that's what we're talking about. My only wife really. She'd—I'd like another but it's really too tough. I'm still, false eye and pasted brow and stitched skin, quite goodlooking by contemporary standards and I dress well and have all these old modeling clothes that I keep clean and pressed, so women are still attentive to me somewhat but my brains give it away. But she wasn't the one who banged me on the head either—wasn't a wife. Young kid did. From my neighbor's hedge. Got out too with only 9 months of seeing a psychiatrist in a comfortable state farm upstate while me—he even learned to read there my lawyer said and grew a few inches—while me, I've got to live with this disfiguring all my life and myself too. This disfigurement. And myself too I have to love with too. Live with but I guess love with too. But my wife. She was a model. Named Donna too. That's what struck me when I heard Beverly's machine. There was love there between us. She walked out on me too after she couldn't take me with half brains and only minor looks left. Looks they corrected a lot but brains they couldn't, but, so, your Donna, with an A?"

"Yes."

"That couldn't be my wife's middle name, the original, her married, but did she have any other names, yours, like Strutstaff, the maiden of my wife's?"

"No."

"Like Katlog then, which was mine when she was my wife last, before she left. But which she never used professionally but changed from Strutstaff to a more modely one: Holmes. No?"

"No."

"Since then she may have changed it to a more modely adult one with an A or any letter, for her career was on the wane. She was getting old, 29, for you see, she always modeled a teen. Katlog's still my name. Thought it good enough for coalmining, good enough for modeling, and mine and my dad's still is."

"No. Donna's always been Donna Akers far as I know. She was once married, I understand, when she was much younger, but must've changed it back to the original."

"No, my Donna wasn't, keep or give away, but your wife have blond hair?"

"She's not my wife and she has very dark hair."

"Long?"

"Curly and short."

"It could've been cut."

"It's been the same length with various styles for 3 years."

"Not wigged which you didn't know about, with or without wig clips sutured to the skin, or dyed black? Strange things can take place when you're away or in the dark or behind bathroom doors."

"Her own color and hair."

"Her breasts then, though they don't seem to be the same people yet. I didn't want to be this free with you, but were hers very large for a model, which means just average for just your average woman-girl?"

"Donna has very small breasts, way below average. She was either ultra-high newspaper and magazine fashion, shampoo or bubbly soap on tv or gloves or stockings or shoes with the top half of her body removed. But rarely in a bathingsuit or bra except when it was marketed to very slim women or she was the before in a bra ad or for an exercising kit or salon when that product or place was supposed to develop the legs, hips and chest. Or as the after for a slimming food or reducing shop when the aim was to decrease these parts."

"There are chemical ways to increase one's bust size, for women, and I guess for men too if you wanted them, but the sequence of events is all turned around where your Donna would have had to increase hers, not my Donna whose I know are nothing but real and for all these years were. No, they aren't the same person, my Donna, my wife, ex, yours. She didn't walk out on me either, vanish on me, for good too. No, she walked out all right, but made no secret where she was till a year ago."

"This Donna's been living with me for 3 years."

"Then it can't be the same person, but for a moment I thought it might. If it was I would have given you information as Beverly asked us to, and if you had found your Donna by now, then given you my best wishes and your Donna a hello. Because I haven't heard from my Donna or of her for a year now, so I don't know where she is either and I'm sure she doesn't want me to. Nor will her friends tell me, though I do see her in ads, but nobody will say where they're made. So it isn't. That's a disappointment. I'm very sorry for you though. I know how it feels in my way and wish you more luck than I."

"Thanks."

"And thank you, sir, for letting me take up your time like this. I wanted to tell Beverly hello also, I always do once a month, which is why I called her, when she spoke about you. It's her birthday."

"Didn't know that."

"Yes, today or one of the days this week or next. I don't know what age."

"Well goodbye."

"I do, but Beverly never wanted me to say."

"I think Donna's told me."

"She shouldn't have—it violates Beverly's faith. But considering our mutual problems, maybe we can meet one day. I'd like it. A mutual talk."

"Sure, let me take your number."

"And my name, though don't if you want. You might much more want to be looking for her most of the time if it happened this soon. At the various terminals. Under different but relatively close names to hers in hotels. Checking unclaimed luggage at these stations' baggage checks. That's what I did, though the 2 cases can't really be compared, as I knew mine had left freely and so only had to find out where."

"No I do and thanks for the advice."

"Great." Numbers. "Call. And even if I hadn't, I hope I haven't been too much."

I call Joanne.

"Hi, where was I?"

"Drugs, but I'd like you to help me do something first."

"Just a sec before it goes away. Drugs. Drugs. Right. The fourth and last of the bad possibilities Donna could have brought on herself and which I flat out reject. She experimented a little. Fact is, we all did, maybe you didn't, sit back, relax, turn on the music we loved to touch, though you never even liked the music much. You were always so impeccably correct and resistant with us."

"Some of the things I like are different from you, not that I didn't respect what you did."

"No you didn't—don't lie. Can't you lower it? Do you have any music more melodic? Why must you get high all the time? you used to say to Donna and us, as if once a week was all the time, and for Mark maybe a little more."

"Respect's maybe the wrong word. Object is what I meant. I didn't."

"You did. You're incredible. It's funny, but more I go into it I don't know what kept you 2 together so long, even if I can understand your worry and loss. Louie, to grab an example, was uncommunicative as anything but at least liked good music and lighting up and dancing and falling down manic and laughs and fun and mad dumb times."

"I did too—the laughs and mad times sometimes—and there was plenty that kept us together. It's just your interpretation against mine."

"Not only mine but others. Maybe not your close friends, what it seemed you had of them, but most of hers. I don't want to name names or try and remember when and where what was said by who, but you disputed me for the truth, you got it, and I'm sorry if it's killing you, especially now. I never should have stepped foot in it. I'm sure it's me now who's violated one of Donna's arch laws."

"Like what?"

"Like arch. Like low. Like I'm being hypothetical."

"Well I'm glad you mentioned it."

"No you're not. You can't stand hearing it. Say you can't. Damnit, who could?"

"Maybe me because so far it's so far from what's what I believe. We had a very nice life together. Had, have, not a life but 3 years. We were companionable and warm, not all the time but almost most. She told me she loved me deeply many times—once just a few weeks ago or so. Not deeply, but that she was in love with me still. She still loved me still. She loved me, plainly. Not plainly but simply. You know what I mean. She simply loved with me, was in love with me, she loved me, told me, last time that time a few weeks ago or so that I said."

"She never said to me she didn't, but that's hardly what I was saying."

"Then I suppose I don't know what you're saying, for it was mostly good between Donna and me. We had arguments, yes, not sharply or so severely where we couldn't speak to each other for days, but we also had lots of good feelings and doings and sharings and regular sex. Great sex sometimes, where there was nothing left of us but sweat. Maybe not that great, but very good. She said she loved it most of those times, those few times when she said she loved it. I did too: said it. Loved it most times. Said that I loved it most times, though more times than she. It was good. We also read to one another at times. From good to great poems and prose and essays—we found that fun. When the place was quiet. Usually late at night. 'Read to me,' we'd say or she'd say 'Tell me what you're getting from that paragraph or page you just read.' She never believed I got anything much out of all the books I borrowed or bought because I could never put in so many convincing words what I was reading or had recently read. And that I only read these books, she said, because other people or critics said these authors or books or both were very good or great. True, most of them weren't very enjoyable or even poetical to read when I wasn't reading them to her or trying to synopsize them for her, and her comprehension was much better than mine, probably by twice. Or in bed we read together or silently to ourselves side by side from different books with classical to modern classical music on or the string quartets which she liked much less. And we also exchanged ideas and viewpoints and stories of the day—talked. We did and also horsed around and kissed and fondled one another everywhere at times. Outside and inside I mean. But mostly indoors, which is what I meant by inside, or outdoors only when we weren't being seen, for we felt it embarrassed most other people and made the lonely ones even lonelier to see us and so forth. And we gave each other massages too. Me mostly to her for she liked or needed them but definitely benefited from them much more than I it seemed."

"In other words, you did just about everything that just about every other unmarried couple your age does who've been together for a few years."

"Maybe more. We slept with our arms around each other in bed, at least when we were drifting into sleep, though not on hot nights like these, and had many of the same interests too. Some books. Films and plays. History. Music. Ballet. Not sports. Some of all those before 'not sports' and also food and wine. No question I drank 3 times as much as she and twice as much as she liked me to and she often criticized me for it. And politics somewhat. Even ethics and economics, as interests, and law, air, oil, art. And other social and cultural problems we were aware of—city things. National and continental and universal things. Things that gummed up the universe or might. Our solar system—what affected it unfavorably and thus our lives. The sun. Like that. We also spoke about having a baby."

"That she never said."

"Some day. An adopted one. In 2 years, if both of us weren't laid off from work, which was 3 when she agreed to it. And maybe in 7 when she was through modeling and if her hoped for movie career didn't pan out and she no longer needed the lower portion of her frame as a showpiece so much anymore, a baby where she gave birth. We even had a contract drawn up about it by a lawyer friend and signed and notarized. Where in exchange for the adopted child I'd build a totally adobe house near the city for her, something she's wanted since she spent a day in one during a vacation when she was 8. By hand—to make and bake the clay myself if that's what goes in adobe. I'd find out. From books. I'd fly to a place where they make them if that's what it takes to learn how. It was all in this contract we've since lost but which I think Donna during some great rage at me, though she never admitted it, ripped up. So there were lots of reasons for us living and staying together and for her not to just pick up without a word to anyone and go."

"I never said no. Maybe I was wrong. I probably am but I don't think I was finished talking before about something else that I was going to relate even something else to, before you went into all that. Drugs. Because let me give you the latest poop about my brother Tom."

"About Donna and him?"

"Donna and Tom? That always seemed smooth, if that's what you mean. No, and excuse me, but they for the short time they saw each other acted with no hiding of displays of affection to anyone except maybe you. But this is about him not concerning her problems for a change. Your phone tapped? Big deal. If it is and mine both, what I wouldn't want the cops to know, half the force probably already does. And about themselves and their comrades, let them know, not that it'll right things to any good. That brother of mine, when the cops came here—I didn't tell you this yet?"

"No."

"To check him out because you gave them his name about Donna. We'll forget you did that and what Tom thought about my friends after that and Mark about you. Well, when the cops came here, they immediately recognized Tom but didn't say anything. The 2 cops and he just winked. What are they I thought, all fairies who go to the same bar? No, Tom told me later, these 2 cops are on the take from him every month. It was all a coincidence. They're not only in Narcotics but citywide patrol once a week in unmarked cars. My brother grows, sells and exports the stuff, which not only was he keeping the news from us but also the goods. When he told Mark and me that we said 'Hey man, you just push your ass out of here. You're a goddamn whore making us pay the inflated street price for it all these years and probably for much of your own sugared down and occasionally poisoned stuff, when from you with all the lodgings and homecooking we've given you not to mention introductions to our best lady friends and unlimited phonecalls, we should've been getting it cleaned and free.' He said he never wanted to get us involved—catch that cock and horsecrap story. And with the cops now knowing his living space, they'll be traipsing around here for a little extra and maybe with a few cops from this new precinct just so nobody should feel excluded, so he had to move out anyhow. But I'm beginning to think he's a born liar and never paid off anyone but did deal big and they knew him because they'd arrested him once and he moved because this place with all the cops that might be coming around had become too hot. Anyway he's gone and didn't say where and I'm still so pissed that I doubt I'll ever want to know."

"One more thing, Jo. I was wondering if you can help me out today."

"Money? I think we can lay a little on you."

"With Donna. I need someone to go around with her photos to the various terminals and such while I call the hotels to see if she was there or still is. Maybe something went with her mind that we don't know about, or if you want to phone the hotels while I—"

"I can't with either. Lunchtime now so everyone's out and they forgot to close down the switchboard as they usually don't forget to do to control outgoing calls, but otherwise this place is a prison. You heard—these cheapskates even put meters on the typewriters so we can't write personal letters on our breaks and we now need badges, and for our visitors elevator passes to get upstairs, which they claim was because women were getting raped by trespassers and hot water coolers and typewriters had disappeared. And the gist of it also is that I still after all this talking to you don't think Donna's missing in any kind of way, overnight craziness or swiped off the street. I think she's really off on a great adventure somewhere, traveling or otherwise, which would've been ruined by planned routes and timetables she thought. Donna's the type to do that without telling anyone or giving a clue, not that she's done it before where anybody I know knows of it and even if I'm the only person who might believe she did, though I think I've thought about her thinking process more and know her better than anyone including you and her father combined. It was in her all the time, even if she never expressed a wish for it, so if you don't mind, this is my attitude about her and I'm going to sit this one out."

"But if you do hear from her, you'll call?"

"Not if she tells me not to."

"Has she?"

"You think I'd be bullshitting you along like this for so long if she had?"

"What should I think now? If I do call you back and you try to get rid of me quick or just give me a few minutes, will it mean you've talked to her and she said not to tell me?"

"What are you talking about? She hasn't called. I haven't talked to her. Don't accuse me that I have. But if she does and tells me not to tell you, I'm not sure what I'll say to you to make you not know. Maybe I would bullshit you along like I didn't do all of before. Maybe I'd have Mark answer the phone at home and at work I'd refuse all your calls. Maybe I'd be brief to the point of a single monosyllable or pretend I'm too sick or loaded to talk but with such good acting that you'd never know I was not. Or maybe I would be sick or loaded and where Donna's also called me and said to never tell you or maybe to tell you but being so sick and loaded I'd forgotten she did to the point of never remembering again or even that she called at all. That could happen. I've gotten stinking blind sometimes. But there's my boss's boss glowering at me again so I've got to go."

"Joanne, I'm not satisfied. Did or didn't she call?"

"No." Hangs up.

I call Betelvine. "She's not here. You from her agency?"

"No, just a good friend. I only want to know if you've seen her today or anytime in the last few days or know anyone who has."

"Why should I tell you?"

"Because I already told you—I'm a good friend of hers."

"You're a good friend, I'm a good friend, but if I called you, good friend, would you be so disposed to answer everything I asked about her because I said I was a good friend too?"

"If you also said you were Art Alimin and lived with her for 3 years in apartment 4W at 16 East 12th Street and knew that she modeled for the Tri-Age Bodity Agency and Beverly Windograde was her representative there and Maurice McElmor the male model she felt most complemented her on couple shots. And you could prove she was booked for a shampoo and cap shoot with the celebrated Betelvine at noon today and her hourly rate is 75 per and that she has a blackhead on her back that she's never been able to find time or courage to get excised and that during the session if her bare back's being snapped she covers this blackhead with something called Dermoknack. And that she never removes her silver waist chain except for modeling sessions when the photographer doesn't want the chain used. And that you also knew Beverly's unlisted home number and can describe her last 3 hairdresser styles in the past 2 weeks and know that she has a miniature schnauzer who she pedals to work with her every day in a plastic bicycle basket and takes on out-of-town trips in a portable schnauzer house though she leaves the bike behind and she also agents for this schnauzer who gets 25 an hour but a 100 for tv though no residuals like regular models do and so forth, yes, I'd answer you, wouldn't you to me? Because all I'd be asking you is if you've seen Donna today or lately or know anyone who has, not if you know if she's been sleeping with anyone I don't know about or if you had once been instrumental in arranging the sale of a stolen stereo to her at way below list price."

"I'm a photographer, not a metaphoricist or whatever that practitioner of semantics is, so I'll solely say to you that I haven't seen Donna since our last photographic session more than a week ago. Waterproof stockings if I haven't forgotten. And why should I have? I've my own friends. Donna's only a toiler to me, no social events. Though she'll be a nontoiler soon or un or whatever the negative prefix is or reverse word for a worker or antonym who's been deprived of the right to work at his or her chosen vocation or chore because of unwarrantable tardiness or tarriance or just plain unpreparedness and incompetence, if she continues to pull tricks like this with me. Time's wasting and I pay penthouse rents for my duplex studio and this is a double session as you so correctly stated—shampoos, and hats that'll make her ravishing head look hydrocephalic despite my most earnest professional efforts to offset that. And I've 2 assistants here and a tub with a ton of soap bubbles rapidly unbubbling and a photo lab on extortionate standby, as both sets of contact sheets have to be in tomorrow morning."

"You see, Mr. Betelvine, she hasn't been seen by anyone for 4 days—that's why I called."

"Hasn't been seen my eye. You speak to Beverly?"

"Yes. All she said was Donna's scheduled with you around noon."

"I'm telephoning her now too. If Donna's not here in one hour and Bodity can't come up with another geek with her hair, ears, eyes, complexion and legs all jelled into one by 3 o'clock today, I'm suing that scrawny bitch and Beverly for all the money it's costing me to wait and to create a new ton of soap bubbles plus what I might lose on these 2 ads and for whatever else I can get because of denigration of character or defamation or whatever the goddamn germane word or applicable adjective or phrase is in my case."

"If I see Donna I'll tell her."

"If you only first see or speak to her an hour from now, also tell her to kiss my ass and get lost."

"That wasn't necessary."

"But suitable because she's screwing up my entire schedule."

"Maybe I didn't make clear what I was saying about her before or you wouldn't be talking like that. Has Donna ever been late with you?"

"No and for good reason."

"That's what I'm saying. Far as I know, she's always been prompt and conscientious, with me and her work. So something has to be wrong. For if she was late or couldn't show, we both know from our experience with her that she would've called you by now or had someone call if she was delayed with something really bad or couldn't get to a phone."

"Donna's never been late because I laid down the law to her agency long before she started modeling for me. That law has never been changed or improved on and goes as such. The advertiser hires me, not the model. I receive a generous fee and contact the agency of my choice for the model I believe will be most perfect for the product and shots. That was the preamble, now for the meat of the piece. The model can refuse to model for me of course. That's her business. But if she does consent then she must have an absolute foolproof excuse for being more than an hour late or why she came to the shoot in the wrong hair style or makeup or shoes that I asked for or in a poor working state or she or he, whether 7 months pregnant or a cripple or decrepit derelict for an anti-smoking or pro-automo accident ad or your child in diapers to my own greatgrandma, will never work for me again. If 2 or more models from the same agency of whatever sex, age, state or persuasion break one of these rules with no foolproof excuse in the course of a year, I blacklist that agency for half a decade. I've been given that power as law establisher and carry-outer because of my comparatively reasonable rates and recognized skills as photographer and administer and because every one of my advertising contracts over the past 20 years has been fulfilled on time or no more than 50 minutes late, and never more than one of these 50 minute or less misdemeanors with any one advertising agency in a year."

"I'm sorry you feel that way about Donna, for I know she needs the work and never once complained about modeling for you. But if you hear from her, could you please tell her to call Art right away."

"Go kiss my ass too."

"I'm serious."

"I'm supposed to be not? Oh god. World's coming to an end for me again. —Gavin, get me a gun. I mean a gin. A triple again." Hangs up.

Gabe. Not in. Gabe again and again, not in. "Operator, could you dial this number? Maybe the party's home and I'm connecting into the wrong line." Not in. Information gives me same number I've been dialing. Information again for Gabe's police station. I get the townhall switchboard, ask for the police, wonder to someone "if an officer couldn't run over to Gabe Akers' place on Stele Street to see if anything might be wrong with him, for he's not answering his phone when I don't know where he could be if he's not in. I'm a friend of a relative—his daughter."

"Donna?"

"You know her?"

"Know her? Went to school with her, public through high. We were pals. Donny and Don. My first daughter's even named after her, though my wife doesn't know it, as it was actually named after my dad Donald senior but she turned out to be a girl. Beauty queen of the town and county Donna was and probably the state if she wasn't so flat and tall before it became allowable and then the whole national pageant if she had made the state, which she should have. I remember her possible competitors that year, nationwide. Nothing compared to Donna and none of her talent too. She ventriloquized—a fantastic act."

"Didn't know that."

"Puppet on her lap—yap yap. She could throw her voice 2 inches to 22 feet. Broke everyone up, Donna in her tux, puppet named Pip, though it was a young lady same age and double for Donna other than for her exaggerated long legs and chest and ears out to hear and unbridled red hair. And sometimes another one on Donna's other knee named Pet—a double for me including crewcut and buckteeth, who as a duo used to knock people out of their seats. She even got Pet and Pup engaged on stage, which we never got any kind of way. Even had them have a baby out of wedlock, which was wicked then—a half pink and blue egg that dropped out of Pup's rear most performances to split open into quads and other times out of Pet's mouth where it quickly popped back when he showed surprise. But that was then. The quads weren't manipulated puppets by the way— more like stillborn. How is she? I haven't seen her for years."

"Not so hot. She's been working a lot, modeling, doing pretty well, trying to get into movies, nothing with puppetry or dummies I think you mean—you're an officer?"

"Third in command."

"Well she disappeared 4 days ago, either on her own or snatched off the street somehow and hasn't been seen since. Gabe—"

"Hold off. Donna?"

"Yes."

"What do you mean yes, yes? Snatched off what street? Where you phoning from?"

"The city."

"But I knew her. Went through public school and high. She's like the biggest thing in my life except perhaps my wife. Donny and Don or Don-Don and Don, though our names were an accident and other than for our hairline and height looked nothing alike. My first child after her. Like the biggest thing to come out of this town as we're that small. Her magazine snaps up on store walls with the chief of state's. I was her first sweetheart, she similar for me. We used to eat over each other's houses every other supper and went on weekend mountain climbing hikes. What's wrong with you people? Not that it's not happening here too, but not off the streets like you. In the homes where it belongs—not that I'm condoning it anywheres, but at least inside families it's understandable to a degree. But on the streets you can still walk untroubled here without muggings and gang fights or riots most nights. No riots any nights. But Donna? Good god, goddamn."

"Take it easy. It's only a possibility. No, more than that—I think it happened. The police and other people say she just picked up and left, though I don't see how. Maybe you can advise me. All her stuff's here. Her career. Bankbook, passport, heirlooms, photo composites, written down past life. And we were close, but she knew all she had to do if she wanted to go or split from me for good was say so and that would've been enough. But Gabe, her father—"

"I know who he is."

"Of course."

"Good god, man, that beautiful moose used to cook for me, gave me my first drink, treated me to restaurants, taught me how to shoot and rebuild my first motorcycle and car. He's a giant in my life, discounting his size. Taught me competitive wrestling and boxing and weightlifting and all the old martial arts besides."

"I'm glad to know he was so versed in those, for he came to the city last night and when I went to the bus terminal to meet him because he wasn't feeling well—"

"What's wrong?"

"Felt faint he said on the phone. I'm sure it was all emotional over Donna."

"Because if anyone ever did anything heinous to him or cheated him out of his dough, I'd beat his brains in if Gabe couldn't."

"Anything's possible here but I'm sure it was only because he was so worried over what I said about Donna being gone."

"He's an old guy. Telling him wasn't wise or nice."

"I held back for 2 days. But what can I say? He's her father and perceptive, so he gradually caught on no matter how hard I lied and then pumped it out of me."

"Still—"

"Still, please, let me get to it, I don't mean to be rude to you but he wasn't at the terminal and hasn't contacted me or answered his phone since. Only since late last night, but I'm worried about him almost as much as about Donna."

"Maybe he's taking in one of your restaurants or shows or wanted to get laid. —No really, don't be so idealistic, sit in everyone's corner for a change. Because the city's a big place to enjoy getting lost in and after a while he might have called someone and found out much more than you—where she is and feasibly that they'd also been told she didn't want you to know."

"People have mentioned that possibility—about her."

"Or else he got tired or sick of waiting for you—maybe from being in that terminal if they still haven't mopped it up, or the bus fumes or human smells. You check your hospitals?"

"I'll call the hospitals, for both of them, though for Donna a little I already have. But I'm sure he would've called me to say he wasn't going to be at the terminal, or at least called later to say why he hadn't been there or called. For one thing, he was very considerate."

"He could be an inconsiderate fucker of the worst order, so let's not embroider anymore about Gabe. Great as he was he was also a pill. He invariably showed up late and did things for his own doing only, just like everybody, and half the times didn't give a lingering piss for your feelings. But the good things overpowered the bad by tons in him and so you put up with and inhibited a lot if you wanted his company, which I did."

"Well to me he was always considerate."

"He also could have forgotten to call you. He's old. Or maybe he reached Donna and she told him not to get hold of you for her own reasons. Maybe she had damn good ones."

"She had none or ones so urgent or turbulent to skip off like that and keep it from me why. Believe me, he either went home by bus or got sick and is in the hospital or something awful, though what I don't know."

"You call your police?"

"About him? No. First—"

"First call your police. Maybe they've a directive on him."

"First I—"

"Now you listen to me, bud. Your name is what?"

"Art Alimin."

"Address and phone number?"

"16 East 12th Street. 324-1279. I can give you the code too."

"I know your code. Let me tell you something, Alimin. 2 A's?"

"Ali with an i and min like the min in minute hand."

"I'm more concerned over Gabe than anyone is including Donna. I see him almost every day, know all his habits. In the winter in my patrol car I see him trying to walk on the ice or over the snow banks, I stop and help him or drive him where he's going and sometimes back. He's been like a father to me in every way, the shits and the greats. He's an institution in this town besides. Besides, the way I knew Donna. They go back ages, the Akers. To the invading natives. To maybe before that. It's been said they interbred with the few aborigines left and some winters maybe even with animals to survive. They came over on wooden boats and several of them, Gabe's said, on rafts. They set up everything in town, built the first post roads and made all the bylaws. His family and one other who the Akers knew in their mutual dukedom somewhere over one of the seas when they were peasants and serfs and slaves. I love this man. So don't tell me what you'll do first or what I should. She left, I stayed. You worry about her and I'll take care what should be done with

Gabe. First off I'll drive to his place. I'll look through every window, search the surrounding area if I have to, open his door and go in if he still keeps it unlocked, something I've cautioned everyone in town not to except the new thieves who've recently moved in around here, but the oldtimers won't give in. While I do this you contact your police and tell them what has or hasn't happened with Gabe and say his community's police force and particularly Sergeant Payyurs there has been informed of the case and is looking into it. If you don't do what I say, I'll drive to the city in the next few days and break in your face. If anything's wrong, then hopefully your police will know. If anything isn't, I'll find out and get back to you if that's what Gabe wants me to do. If he doesn't, then I'm talking to you now for the last time, Art, unless you phone me about something unrelated to his case or you're driving through the area and I happen to stop you for a moving violation. Now get to it as you said."

"Thanks. That was all I was after—some action."

"Don't thank me so soon. Because you better be equal to receiving my equivalent thanks to you."

I call the city police and tell the officer about Gabe. She says "You check with his home town force yet?" I tell her about Sergeant Payyurs and she says "You tell him that one missing day at sea even in a hurricane wind scale of 17 isn't sufficient to think a tiny tanker's sinking. And if Mr. Akers hasn't been certified by the court or court-authorized psychiatric decrees to be incapacitatingly enfeebled or deranged and so long as he hasn't broken bond or absconded with anyone's money or done anything criminal in an illegal sense and is paid up on his legitimate bills, he's got every right to take off for as long as he likes and go wherever he wants to except countries our federal government expressly objects to without telling a soul. If his private police force is still that hyped up about him, tell them to give me a ring."

I call back Payyurs. His townhall switchboard operator says "I saw him leave 3 minutes ago—I'll tie you in."

"You caught me in my cruise car," Donald says. "What's news?"

"The police here say Gabe's got the right to disappear for as long as he wants, just as they said about Donna, and if you still want to speak to them, here's the number."

"No wonder you have so much crime. I'm driving to Gabe's place this minute. Looks peaceful from here. Chipmunk on the loose, wash whipping away on the line, nextdoor neighbor's horse feeding off the leaves on Gabe's trees. There's his mailbox. Hold on, I'm opening it. Few bills. Seed package—probably fall lettuce and snow squash. Weekly supermarket penny-saver enumerating expensive bargains he'll never buy. Picture postcard from ole Martin, our gunsmith here, from over the border where he's vacationing, showing their battle ready lady sailors on parade. I got the same card and probably the same message: 'How they hanging, sharpshooter?' though I won't look at his to corroborate that. Couple letters. What do you know, both from Donna."

"Open them."

"Can't do that. No warrant to and Gabe will kill me even if the judge issued me one."

"She's been missing 4 days. The letters may explain where or why and something about Gabe being gone too."

"Maybe it's okay. I do in emergency situations have the prerogative to commit some rash acts. You got that, Madelis?—she's the switchboard eavesdropper here. If Donna's really missing, these envelopes allegedly sent by her could contain ransom notes."

"Policework's police work," a woman says, "and have I once breathed a word about anything you might've done?"

"Got to do it carefully so I can seal them back intact. Also have to remember how the paper inside is folded when I open it so I can fold it back exactly too. Gabe's on the ball and might get leery if he sees her letter folded the opposite way it always comes, that is if she does it the same way every time. If she folds it any old way every time but without even accidental exactness, my precious efforts here will be a big waste. What's that? No, just a hawk flapping in and out of Gabe's barn and that horse yodeling. I love my old lady too. Okay. I'm extracting a pair of folded up sheets of paper out of the back of the envelope. Folded part corresponds in its placement in envelope to envelope's back flap. Paired sheets folded in 3 parts, top to bottom and bottom part over top. Try and remember this for me, Art, in case I forget when I stick them back. Seems to be a letter. Handwritten, unlike the envelope which was typed. I'm unfolding the first fold on top. What do you know. First sheet facing me at the top of the first unfolded part says 'Dear Daddy' and is dated 4 ... 5 ... 6 days ago. They are though postmarked same time on the same day in your city. Could have crawled here in that time or not quite. I don't think I should read it."

"Please."

"Gabe finds out—he's still a powerful mother you know. Can wallop me clear over a goat with just one blow and knows I won't poke back."

"I'll take full responsibility for opening and reading them if I can."

"Excuses are illfit expressions for whatever that commonplace is—lack of confession of the law or some such hogbosh. You just don't know anything about my opening this letter, you got?"

"Yes."

"Tell him or anyone and I'll drive to the city just to knock your front teeth in if you still got them. You too, Madelis. I'm not threatening you bodily of course but you won't say anything now that we know it's not ransom notes—not even to your 3-legged physician friend in the first town over the mountain. Not even on his postcoital couch when his soulwife's out or via your table rappings if you die and he calls you back to speak."

"If you don't mind, Donald. What you say is unfair, absolutely absurd, not true, and even if it were, crude and uncalled for on the 2-way when a third person can overhear. Besides, my ears have been clogged throughout to whatever you've said and I'm buzzing off."

"Madelis? —She's gone or isn't, as she can switch off without a sound. Okay, I'll read it. If you're still there, Madelis, remember this is serious lawful policework and also what I know about you and yours and his and even her his which I don't even think you, he or she knew about. It's a long letter, slim margins and tiny script. Well look it here, my name at the bottom of the page."

"Start from the top."

"But I'm anxious to know what she has to say about me after all these years. 'Why for instance even Donald Payyurs did you take such a dim view of all through pre and regular school when he of all people thought the most highly of you? It was the same with every boy and man I introduced you to since I was 5. None were smart or good enough—horse manure if you'll excuse me—not for me but for you, and not the manure not for me and forget my excuse me, but the smart and good enough for you. Besides that—over' meaning next page. Next page is more of the same. Now that's something I never knew. Be that as it may, Gabe will never find out I now do. But to begin. Window up, to keep in the air-conditioning. Energy crisis and all—this is me, Donald speaking—I've gotten too used to it. 'What,' she says after her Dear Daddy, 'is it you're so afraid I'll do, or is it your you're'—which are her words, probably written too quick to correct it and maybe the same for sending it out, 'afraid'—the 'your you're' before it—'of me in every way and just can't get up enough guts to recognize it, which only increases—oh I hate the word increases—aggravates is more like it. Intensifies, heightens'—I hope you know all this is Donna speaking, up until the end of my interjection now—'deepens, soups up your latent, hidden, maybe untraced and explored'—she has a hyphen before the explored—'but always underlying anger, rancor, hate and rage—oh the hell with it, what's the use?' and 3 or 4 exclamation points after the word use but no question mark, the periods underneath tearing straight through the page. What do you make of it? To me she was always sweet as can be and I never thought they got along any ways but great. Madelis, you know? She's on her toes also—downright discerning—and knows everything about this and the surrounding towns. What a time to goad her off the phone or make her think she has to pretend she's not there. Madelis, if you're there, I apologize and will positively, not on my hands and knees because I'm in the front seat with reams of ammunition and supplies in this cramped car—keep my trap shut about everything I so unwisely said about you, so please come back and speak. And it was also dumb of me to talk in front of Mr. Alimin, who I know has his own problems and won't be saying a word about you too."

"Of course I won't."

"'How come each time I ask you for a favor or little advice,' Donna says, 'you have to swamp me with your remonstrances and bile about my evil degenerate etcetera detestable life when I've always always'—first always once and second twice underlined—'let you lead yours whatever way you liked—crazy, selfish, oblivious, insensitive, contemptuous, disreputable, discreditable, sanctimonious, shameful, base, squalid and vile.' No sir, no ma'am—he's never going to see this. I'm going to tear it up."

"Don't."

"You know what a letter like this would do to Gabe?"

"It's not your property."

"So what? Lots of things come before that."

"Finish reading it. She might say where she might be in the next few days—some clue, something."

"Suppose he walks up his driveway now and sees me and says what do you have there, son? and I say a letter and he says who from? and I say my brother Hal and he says that's Donna's writing and address typing if I never saw one and grabs the letter from me, forget what he thinks of my opening and reading it and now my lying to him which I've never done, but his reading it himself. Because he's never said anything to me but the kindest most thoughtful just wonderful proud paternal things about her—what a beauty she is and always was and the money she's been able to make off it. And her sorting out the system of your city to turn over one heck of a good life for herself in it and get around cleverly as she does with everybody, whatever like that—and how sharp she is too and that she could fall in a barrel of shit and come up with a gold brick from it, his very words, though he didn't coin them. He loves his daughter like no father I know does. Not like I do with mine and she's barely 5—I've hardly had time to get to dislike her one bit yet. R-r-r-rip. Sound effects to the actual happening of these 2 sheets and envelope being torn in half and now 2 to 7 times to shreds. Out the window they go. Hey look at it snow. Hell, in July—a record even for our cold parts. Latest to date a May 28th fall 15 years ago that stuck and accumulated enough for Donna and I to coast down Boldface Rock bareassed but my midriff warm along with our best couple friends stacked on the next sled, another pair making it precociously then on all fours."

"You really tore it up?"

"You need one of those mammoth fishing nets a square acre long to pick the pieces up."

"You remember seeing anything else on it she wrote?"

"'How come, papa, you acted the same estranged hateful way with ma and grandma? How come you won't let me alone and never did them all your grown years and from what they said, also when you were young? How come you can't find one nice thing to say about anyone that truly comes from the inside rather than from your flat put-on nice guy pose? How come you continue to write me those odious letters when you say you've sent the last one or phone me with your poisonous remarks when you said just a week ago and before that just a week and a week before that that you'll never phone me again? How come you've always set everyone against me and me against—oh forget that. How come you persist in this shitty way? How come—no. I'm trying to be constructive. Why is it—enough. Goddamnit—when will you finally say for the final time I don't like this girl and she doesn't like me and let's face it I detest her almost as much as she loathes me though probably more and in fact she is no longer my daughter, that's right, and I no longer will have or want to have and won't have a thing to do with her forever and anon and amen. When? Why for instance even Donald—but why after all that now bring him up? But yes, why even Donald Payyurs did you take such a dim view of all through' and so on, over, next page, more of the same but not much—enough, kiss off and signs it Donna. No love, bests, yours sincerelys. That's it. Now I'm ripping it up."

"Wait. I didn't hear it all nor catch everything you said. Photocopy it for me first."

Sound of paper tearing. "Out the window just as I prophesized. Breaking the highway litter law here but in this case I'd arrest myself if I didn't."

"And the second letter?"

"Should throw it out in shreds without even reading it but

won't. I'm opening it. One page, folded same 3 part way, not that you have to remember the unfolding details for me anymore. Says . . . 'Sorry'—no dear whoever—'for the things I said and way I said them in the last letter or letter you'll next read and probably got with this, as they'll have been slipped in the same post office slot only a half hour apart. But I had to say it, meant most of it, doubt if anything will change much between us because of it but, well, hope this letter gets to you before or after it but gets there if the other did, though hope it doesn't if the other didn't. If I don't hear from you in a week from today, which I'm jotting down now in my mnemonic pocket day-timer for next Tuesday at around noon o'clock, I'll phone. I'll start off with my normal nice daughterlike voice saying hi dad or hello, just in case you didn't get either letter or just the one I'm all but totally apologizing for here. Which is a possibility—losing them both—having lost so much mail to and froing this year, sometimes because I forgot to mail them and dumped or washed the coat or pants they were in or just forgot to put on stamps, which this time I can't recall if I had with the first letter, being in such a rush to get it mailed. It's true I meant to hurt you and still do somewhat but not in a letter or in that particular rabid malicious way, honest as it may have been, though who knows even there. If we could only sit down and talk things out rationally, over coffee or tea, beer even, stupid as you usually get on 2 glasses of it, but you won't hear. But from now on ease up on me just a little, daddy dear, okay? Love, D.' This one I wouldn't rip up if I hadn't the first, so out it goes."

"All she said?"

"It." Rips. "Snow, breeze blowing it down the road. 2 storms in one July day—a record even for May. First one's already in other people's fields and yards and sailing to the hills. Flying—ships sail. I'm driving up to Gabe's house now. Car's stopped. I'm in front. I'm getting out to scout around and go in. Wait for me on the phone."

Doorbell. I cover the receiver and yell "I'll be there in a minute please."

"He shouldn't have done what he did," Madelis says.

"What?" I say to her.

"It's Mrs. Lessafor from the second floor, Mr. Alimin. I read your—"

"Shouldn't have," Madelis says. "He can get canned. And now knowing it and not tattling, me too."

"—and heard your messages last night and wonder if there's something I can do."

"I'm on the phone with the police, Mrs. Lessafor, so can I get back to you soon?"

"My interrupting anything?" Madelis says.

"Neighbor."

"I'll wait too."

"I also brought food for you—soup and my homemade bread. Know it's hot out too much for that soup and my kitchen's boiling from the stove and oven heat both, but I didn't have fruit to make a real cold fruit soup like I like to on summer days and no store beats my bread, but maybe it will do for you—they're good."

"Thank you."

"No thanks necessary. Only a few slices and a little in the pot enough for 2. Thought you must need something shaken up with all you must be and gone through and maybe still do. No word on that poor girl?"

"None. And it's very kind of you, Mrs. Lessafor. Sorry for the troubles I might've put you through last night and with the food. Leave it—"

"No troubles. I don't sleep anyway and made enough to save most of that bread and soup for myself too."

"Thanks. Leave it by the door. I'll phone you when I'm through."

"I haven't one."

"I'll come down."

"That would be nice. But me leave it by the door for the dogs to paw over and cats to kick and eat not to say people's feet? No thank you."

"I'll only be a few minutes. If the soup's real hot the heat of it should keep the animals away."

"And the bread? It's only warm."

"Maybe you better take the bread with you."

"I will. I'll give you 5 minutes. If you're not down there by then, I'll come up and get the soup which won't be too hot for the animals anymore, so you'll know when you open your door and don't see it, where it is. I'll also leave the pot cover on top. Don't forget to remember it's very hot, soup and pot. I'll leave the potholders on the pot handles it's so hot, just if you don't remember how so, but bring them back with the pot when you're through. In fact, bring the holders back before. They're my only ones. In fact, when you—"

"Doesn't she ever shut up?" Madelis says.

"—pour before what's in my pot into your own if you have one and bring down to me my clean pot and cover and holders all the same time, okay? It's an old-fashioned ironware you can't buy anymore except the newest kind at the most expensive stores."

"Right. Goodbye."

"So all that plus—"

"Alimin?" Donald says.

"Hold on."

"—should now take you pouring and cleaning and all 6 to 7 minutes till I see you, Mr. Alimin, or for me to run back up to see if the dogs and cats got at my soup and soiled the floor. Goodbye."

"I was talking to a neighbor. Go on."

"Gabe's door was open. Place was ransacked—"

"In fact, better I take the pot with me. They sell the old ones in contemporary antique shops for fortunes now and it would break my heart to lose it. Pick it up with me downstairs."

"I will."

"—plenty of semi-valuables were taken that I knew he had."

"Anything about Donna?"

"Nothing. His radio. Portable broiler she gave. Windup mantel clock from his family's year one. Drawers, closets—you know the route—and orthopedic mattress stood up and slit open and even a smoldering cigarette filter in a saucer when Gabe never smoked and wouldn't let it in his house, plus a chewed up wad of gum big as a golfball on the floor when he never chewed anything but food. Little muddy footprints and big ones both with perforated sneaker holes—man and child, boy or girl. So the jokers were just here, but no Gabe. I'll call your cops from the car. His being gone could be innocent. Good thing you got me here though, not that I stopped anything but some smoking and chewing and maybe their demolishing the whole house. They must have seen me parked by the mailbox and darted into the woods with their goods and by now are probably in their car on one of the logger roads in there heading for either of the highways they can come out on in a dozen different places on the other side. Say, it's been great."

I hang up, run to the door, soup's gone—"I got them down here," Mrs. Lessafor yells walking from the third to second floor. "I thought I told you. Already the dogs were—"

"Forgot, I'm sorry, don't know where my mind's going, I was suddenly hungry, thank you," and go in and call back the townhall switchboard. "This is Art Alimin from before—Madelis?"

"You going to let on I was snooping on you 2?"

"No. I thought you had something else to tell me about Donna or Gabe."

"Nothing. I liked her. Great little girl. Little? Actually I'm the younger and foot shorter but she was always much younger in looks and personality than me. What I mean is always usually bouncy and chattery with a head on her while I hadn't. Skinny—obese. High liver upper—low. Other unlikenings. But keep searching—something seems screwy as you say. Her. Gabe. God. Cops—if it was their own kin or lost dog missing or a promotion or pay raise, they'd be hopping. Otherwise—got to do it most yourself. But they're really not all bad, cops, and get lethargic with the job like everyone, having worked with them so long and just in case someone's now listening in on me."

"If you—"

"If I see her, sure, honey, anything, or Gabe, I'll let you know. You're in the book under your name, right? There can't be too many of you on East 12th Street. Any word I get—even to top secret highly classified rot—I'll phone if Don doesn't. He had no right—you heard him. Likeable as he is, it wasn't true and he had no right besides about my psychic friend. I tit for tat in my own hurtless way, though don't tell him you spoke to me about this or anything but hello Madelis, get me Sergeant Payyurs please, or whatever news I might get from now on you won't. Not that I'm promising I'll get any news. I probably won't. I in fact know I won't. Certainly nothing that could help find her but only Gabe. But you never know. Bye."

I hang up. Receiver falls off the hook and the cat scratches me when I'm picking the receiver off the floor. Reached its paw out I thought just to get petted and I started to, holding the receiver and with its paw still up, when it scratched. Hand's bleeding. Cat leaps on the night-table I'm sitting beside and raises and shakes the same paw at me. "You bastard," slamming down the receiver and pushing the cat off. It runs out of the room, comes into the bathroom where I'm washing the cut and sticks its paw in my pants leg and tries to pull it out of the cloth but can't. I take its paw out and pick the cat up to see how long its nails are and then what sex it is but it doesn't seem to have anything to identify it as male or female. It squirms in my hand while I'm looking for this extension or slit by parting its hair around there and then sticks its nails in my shirt nipping my shoulder and again I have to take the paw out of the cloth by hand. "Maybe you're hungry again, that what you're saying with your paw?" and I put it down and in the kitchen open a can of Donna's tuna fish, for I never eat it, and can of evaporated milk I remembered she kept in the back of the top cupboard a foot above our heads so nobody else would use it and which she liked, if there was no fresh or powdered milk, with her morning tea and put both cans on the floor and say "Here kitty kitty, come on boy, nice girl" and the cat runs in wagging its tail and sniffs and seems to inspect both foods before it alternately eats and sips.

I tape a sign above the vestibule mailboxes that says Found: Cat/Black/Can't Retract Paws/Long Wagging Tail Pin-Striped Gray/Call Art/Apt 4W/324-1279/Or Ring Bell Downstairs or my Door. Hang identical signs in the vestibules of the buildings on either side of mine and one on the lamppost in front of my building. Super's wife is coming up the basement steps outside with a large black plastic bag of garbage and says "Sir, nothing to hear for Mrs. Akers so far, Mr. Art?"

"No."

"Anything I do?"

"You want to help me?"

"Yes, want to help, yes."

"You yes no want to help nobody—not I know this man," super says coming up the steps carrying 6 of the filled garbage bags, 3 in each hand.

"Me I help who I want, not you."

"You help bags. Down there 4 more and clean up halls and glass on door and sweep and hose down street with me and we done for day."

"Why you act like this? His wife help us plenty with food and things. With children, when I'm sick, and tell me makeup and hair, she does. Of all new people she nicest we know."

"She not wife of him. Try help and I crack both your legs. You want up his room too?"

"What can I help you, sir?"

"Thanks but I don't want to cause a family dispute."

"Dispute? Fight? Family? Between me, this man, there nothing. Last night he won't let me, tell me stay, but now for her I do."

"I say no, don't, never, do!" Throws his bags to the sidewalk and grabs her arm and pulls her downstairs.

"What's up?" a woman says.

"That guy's wife. My super, who he says, when I'm looking for my own—" but she's too sleazy looking, dirty hair in uncombed knots, fly mostly open, zipper broken, supermarket cart loaded with old clothes and junk and she smells, though she might be peddling the stuff to secondhand stores. "Nothing, forget it" and I go in my building. Sign above the mailboxes is gone. I go in the other buildings' vestibules. These signs gone too. One on the lamppost too, when I'm sure it was there when I ran past the post to go into both buildings' vestibules. "Lady—excuse me—my sign here. You see it? Take it? Anyone who did?"

Shakes her head, pulls out a pants pocket, takes off her hat and shows me the inside, points to the cart, then to the corner, pumps her arms back and forth like a runner, goes back to rummaging through the bags the supers just threw out, finds a tie, chair for a doll house.

From my building's first floor I yell "Hey. Maybe there's a good reason I don't know of yet for tearing down notes about people, but why the hell cats?" Wait.

Run down the outside basement steps and shake the locked gate which is a couple feet from the super's door while I try to fit my hand through it to ring their bell but can't and say "Either of you, Mr. and Mrs. Edo or your kids, didn't take down my notes about the missing black cat or Donna last night, did you?" and he opens the door and says "Enough, sir, don't trouble us. Too much already with police coming by day past this one and before asking us of you."

"What police? From last night asking you what about me?"

"Me. You. Say who are you. How long here you. Say how you do with Donna. Say we want to ask one more question, super, and then one more. And your wife, super. One more. Why you think I don't want her help your Donna? Shaking my children up. Waking. Young. You seen them young. Bells. Late. Phones on, off, phones on the phone. Saying I want you, super—the police. Where you been this night, all the nights, super?—the police. Saying you both been here only one year and such a good job, super? Where you both been before? Go way. Leave us peace. We run away from one country for this one and still so bad? No. You make too much trouble not good for me, worth for me, be here, this dirty work. No mix us up more or I get very angry. I very big man—you see—tall and quiet, and want very quiet my house."

"I'm sorry. I didn't mean to drag you into this. But do you know who—"

"No, never knew, go away, last time. I have to go upstairs 5 flights and get everybody's garbage now because of you, that's not enough?" and slams his door.

I go into the building west of mine and shout through the lobby door "Anyone here take down a note I taped above your mailboxes 10 minutes ago about a missing black cat?" Building to the east of mine: "Please, anyone take down a note I had above the mailboxes about a missing black cat with a tail striped gray? Does anyone also know, long as I'm here, anything about a Donna Akers who lives next door in number 16? This is important. She's been missing for 4 days. Tall and pretty like a fashion model, short dark hair, usually carries with her a big black leather portfolio like a huge flat attache case. If you do, to any of these questions, could you please phone me, Art Alimin, I'm in the directory, with 2 i's, my last name, in number 16 of this block, right next door to you if you forget, or just my apartment bell, 4W, ring it and I'll run down. If I'm not in, drop a message in my mailbox or try again. Thank you."

I repeat in the other building I was just in the part about Donna and calling or buzzing me or dropping a message in my mailbox and go into my apartment and start calling all the hospitals in the city including the local one I phoned last night.

No Donna or Gabe Akers registered or admitted in the past 4 days every one of them says.

"Any name like that—Acers, Ackers, Bakers, or any Donna or Gabe?" I ask each one. All but one won't tell me or just say no. That one says "Avid Slater?"

"A man?"

"She came in with a coronary yesterday. Has no one, or what we can learn, as she was too paralyzed from the stroke to speak and has no letters or address book and none of her neighbors know much about her except she goes in and out to shop once a week. Emaciated. Dehydrated. Floor and bed sored. A dozen different diseases gone untreated for years. Been dying in her room for 3 days before someone walked by her window of the hundreds a day who must and peeked inside, or at least the only one to see and say anything about what he saw, and seen her lying on the floor and called the police. Everyone only at home ought to have someone who phones them once a morning at a fixed time and also punctually and maybe every night before bedtime besides, holidays included, and then comes over with the keys if they don't answer, at least when they're that age and if the phoner doesn't live too far away."

"Good idea. And I don't think Mrs. Slater is one of the ones

I'm looking for, though the names are close, with those 2 strong a's in the first and last like Akers and Gabe."

"Too bad. For starting in a few tomorrows she could use someone to know and visit her and maybe later to phone her like I said, though not if her cords stay paralyzed. The nurses tell me she's very cooperative and despite her hardships, quite cheerful and nice."

"Does that mean she'll live?"

"Does it mean she'll live? Will Avid live he's asking me. —This man, who I don't know. Never knew her but something about if we admitted his sister or wife or husband or child. Let me tell you, my friend—"

"I'm sorry, I shouldn't have asked—it's none of my business."

"No, listen to me, my friend, listen. That will she live business isn't in my hands or yours for us to say."

"I understand. Her doctors—"

"I'm not even talking about theirs, competent as we got. But before you run off, you want to come visit her now that you know? None of her neighbors will. Maybe they hated her or for other reasons, like she's too old or like the landlord does, want her out because she's paying such cheap rent and doesn't mix, but just someone to be there at bedside once a day around mealtime might be good for her recuperative spirits. And all our aides and volunteers including salaried me during my hard-won late afternoon breaks are much too busy feeding and cleaning the patients to have time for idle chitchat and in Avid's case, just reading something to her or turning on the telly and holding hands."

"If I wasn't so busy trying to find these 2 people—"

"Do one good turn like this and you'll see how your misfortunes change."

"It's not that I don't want to. But being or even just walking into a hospital lobby can be an extremely emotional thing for me. My father died in one."

"Better than in a gutter or dreary nursing home if what he died in wasn't."

"But my brother and mother too. One after the other in less

than 3 years and each from a different disabling disease. That was my whole family and I was also with each one before the doctors sent us or me out of the room and pulled out the plugs. So you can see what I mean, not that I wanted to fill you in on me, but I will write it down. Avid Slater. Older person. Aldoroon General on Glen and Broome. To try and visit her after the next few days."

"Try not to think about it too long. If you do come, see me at the reception desk—Rosalee, I'm a big woman, always a happy flower on my chest and fresh face and dress, from noon to 9 always except Wednesdays."

Phone rings between 2 of these calls. "Hi, is Donna in?"

"No, who is this?"

"By chance did she leave a phone number or forwarding address?"

"No. Nor has she called or been seen by anyone I know for 4 days. She's, what can I say?—lost."

"Like how lost—in a hospital with her head?"

"Missing. Possibly grabbed off the street, maybe worse."

"No, not worse."

"Yes, yes worse."

"Then it's so. Okay, good. I'm glad. Show's over. Not glad she's missing but isn't lying. Oh she'll be found. No worry, I know Donna enough to know—found when she wants to be or it's most important to, right?"

"What makes you think that?"

"Because I'm positive. I think positively. Because I say everything's great, whole world's right, and put my mind to it and get other people to, so nothing bad ever happens to people I know and like. But this'll mean she'll still be handled by us at least. And she's one of our best models. One of the best meaning kindest with the most experience and class but just a mite over her apex, so it'd be a pity to let her go when she still has a couple of good slaving years left. But excuse me, this is Beverly's assistant at Bodity—Eve, you remember me, right?"

"I'm sorry, no."

"All those times I phoned for Bev and said Eve Maluker for Miss Windograde, is Donna Akers by the by?"

"Mustn't've been me."

"And Donna's never mentioned her Eve? Oh, she's in big trouble with me, big. Bev too. I'm hurt, I'm shocked. Really, seriously, I am not, but besides all the trivia I'm talking, who is this, Donna's beau Bob?"

"Art."

"I know. Just slapping back. Though don't hold it against me as my mind's not only working positively for Donna now but you. You see, Bev's away for the week so it was to fall on my unpaid assistant happenstance to give Donna the ax impersonally from Mrs. Bodity herself. You know what I mean with my unpaid joke happenstance and that before latter bit by the by?"

"No."

"Didn't think so. Neither much did I. Just said them because they seemed to sound so erudite and clever, but you thought both latters were jokes that zoomed over your head or maybe you didn't feel you had time to think about them I was barreling along so out of breath."

"Yes."

"Just achecking, my Art. Me, I let nothing go by the by. Say something that sounds fishy or I don't get the drift, then even if it mimics my ignorance and insensitivities, I stop the funeral outright and ask. But you don't. Bev doesn't. Donna does. That says something about her too, right?"

"I guess."

"What does it say?"

"I don't really know, nor do I like being inquisitioned like this."

"Then why'd you say it did? In conversation you just like to get by, right? Get the person off the line quick with no marks made on you. You and Donna are very different. I'd think Bev or Mrs. B would be more your type, since I don't think opposites really attract in humans as they do in physics, do you?"

"Occasionally they do but I don't think it's a basic law of romance or living arrangements."

"Good. Now you're thinking and conversing in common both. Not that you needed to hear that from me and do you think I'm being too personal with you?"

"Not really."

"Yes you do by shovel loads. Just getting by. Trying to keep the car brand new after years of it on the road. Don't wax it in the sunshine, no more than 3 people of medium build in the back seat—you boys, hey you boys there, stop sitting on the fender as I don't want any nicks or dents. But the ax. Way the by I'm through with you now and in my own oblique way, as I don't give them as readily or courageously as I do my opinions and perceptions, apologize."

"Doesn't matter, say what you like."

"Pardon? I'm hearing right? You don't mind me, after I said I'd stop and my oblique apology for saying too much in what I thought was this incredibly distressful time for you, to say what I think about you when I thought you knew it was obvious I didn't really want to? Truth now, yes or no?"

"All I can say is I've several important calls to make, so if anything I don't have the time to argue or listen much anymore."

"And if I said I'd do it quickly?"

"Why would you want to do it at all?"

"Just say if I said I'd do it quickly, would you mind?"

"I'm only interested in what you might know to help me find Donna. But if you have to first say what you think about me to get to it, hopefully quickly though any other way so long as it doesn't take all day, do."

"Well then I think you're an asshole, Art, do you know that? I didn't think it so much before if at all or want to say this but I definitely now think you're an asshole, do you know that? A perfectly round and big accommodating one, the beaut of beauts. You let people say and do what they want with you and make out as if you've a tough hide to it when you don't. Before I thought it a temporary quirk in your personality because of Donna being lost, but I now see it's been there almost forever and won't change except through radical recourse. Now why do you think I know this about you and what gives me the right to feel I can say it and especially on this day?—You also have nothing much to say and maybe you're in the social, emotional and intellectual ways quite shy and infantile and only semi-smart, though go to great pains to pretend you're not. But deep down you're miserable over this awareness of yourself and draw attention because of this mysterious misery which you refuse to reveal the causes of and thus the possible solutions to because you enjoy the attention you get from this misery, as you feel it's the only attention you're worth or can get. —Do you think I'm right in any of this? —Is all this news to you then? —Is there anything you want to comment or quibble over in what I've just said? —Then do you want me to go on or hang up or just stop without waiting for your reply? —Well then, I did think Donna had been dragged off the street or some like crime, though in the end felt everything would turn out okay. Why or how I couldn't say, except I was getting the most positive vibes about her and now know what they mean. For after speaking with you I now see she left on the sly and by surprise because there was no other way to leave without you incredibly upsetting her. Now how about my last remark? —Then how did you feel when I was saying all that? —Then do you now think I'm the perfect beaut of beauts and incredibly wrong in everything I've said? —Then what do you think of my using the word incredibly 3 times in so short a space? —Answer at least one of these questions or I'm hanging up."

"If you want you can use the word incredibly 3 more times and consecutively with no breath stops, but just tell me if you've anything else to say which might help me find Donna."

"All right. No more. I am deaf and dumb struck. Is it clear what I mean by my deaf and dumb struck remark or do you think I'm now resorting to affectedness to get you to answer me? But I said no more so no more. The ax. Ah yes the ax, for picture me giving these instructions to Donna, which I've got written down here. What to do, to say, so forth, how to approach—even my opening pitch, that hello or hi Mrs. Bodity said it'd also be okay to say, is Donna in? For what? To find if Donna isn't playing tricks with Betelvine because she detests his tyrannousness so much and through him us to lose those quote Bodity unquote spectacular accounts? And just Donna's recent arrogance Mrs. B said—showing up late too often or like today, if her being gone criminally isn't so as I think but won't say, not at all. But I better keep my mouth tight as she wants Donna and all her models doing—to act ingenuous and naïve and rebuff their potential Bodity client mashers with greater humor and finesse—for our phones are being tapped by the feds since we began getting lewd calls for a week coupled with firebomb threats."

"I do have these other calls to make, so you through?"

"My feeling is she left not only because your relationship not working, possibly incredibly upsetting her, etcetera, but also because she was mistreated here not only by Mrs. Bodity but most of the account execs and photogs, male and fe both, who dealt with her either like a wooden puppet they wanted to woodenly lay or give out their vituperations to. Take that for 12 years without much bellyaching and I'd think one day you'd wake up and want to run away screaming from."

"If she didn't like it she could've switched agencies or quit permanently and what about her bank savings and check account if she didn't close them and past residuals and personal belongings she left behind?"

"Those are the few things I can't answer yet. But give me time or when we eventually see Donna again, and I deeply feel we will and sense it where she'll be a lot better off financially and looking when we do, that part of it will be explained. Meanwhile I'm glad I can legitimately report back to Mrs. B that Donna's not hiding or off on a grand spree with someone but gone, straight off the face of—even her lover for years says so and the police know, because not only can't I lie if my life or job depended on it but when Donna returns she might want her job back. So if you hear from her today or nearabouts and she's been sleepwalking or waterskiing we'll say, don't tell me, okay? Not that I won't be overjoyed or know it through more extraordinary sources by then, but another thing I can't do to save my life is keep someone's secret."

Donna's savings book is here. I call her bank and the clerk says it's private information whether they've received checks made out in the last few days by the account holder.

"Maybe I'm not explaining myself right. My customers are basically honest or I know them, but this lady, Mrs. Akers—I'm a storekeeper, Bargain Ben's on Nemsen Street—wrote this check for a color tv, big as a small wall, when her brother calls or man saying he's so an hour after she goes and says he's been trailing her all day and saw her go in my store and write a check. But don't deposit it he tells me or deliver the purchase she bought if she didn't take it with her, for her address is false and check's worthless as she has nearly zero in her account. Help me stop her from being put away which is why he's telling me all this he says, for once a month for a few days when the moon is in a certain sign she thinks, she goes on a shopping lark with checks that bounce 8 different ways."

"That's a little different as we do extend a special courtesy to businesses" and comes back and says "This ought to make your day. We haven't received one of Miss Akers' checks for a week. Her brother's in error or whoever's playing a naughty prank on her, since as far as we can see she keeps a scrupulous account, always with adequate funds in reserve and never overdrawn."

I call Curt and he says what's what and I tell him and ask if to save me some time he could phone a number of hotels to see if Donna's been there or is there now.

"No, that'd be too embarrassing, asking after a woman—what do I say when they ask who you are and my business with her and what if she is there and answers or friend of hers does? But also because after thinking it over myself I'm another one who thinks she went on her own too."

"Who else we know does?"

"Friends of yours you'll have to find out yourself who and some personally of mine, excuse me, I spoke to too. One's an assistant d.a. I know from my local bar. God annihilate me first I should appear before him even fighting a traffic ticket when he's juiced. Because all of a sudden divorced also, living alone, one room instead of his usual 6 and no kids now and half his income to them and not used to it so hotheaded as shit—okay, sob story, pickling himself to pieces but still a whiz in his field even when juiced and he says 'Your buddy never got a ransom note, yes?'"

"I didn't."

"That's what I told him, you didn't and he said 'He didn't. They most never do and 3 days or more are up so 99 point 8 chances or almost the same percentage she took off for private reasons her own.' My mother also, excuse me, but we talk on the phone every day and I have to have something to say, she also said the same about my dad. She had to remind me of it because I still hold the illusion they told me then that he was lost a grenade wielding hero in the war. He also went to a movie, was actually seen sitting through 2 double shows and 33 years later to the day Donna was said missing he still hasn't marched home. Main reason she remembers the date so well is it was her birthday, which I forgot again this year, and god get me for that one too, and that movie he sat through was the one he promised to take her for her celebration to that night. Now was he knocked off? she asked me. Or swallowed up by the sidewalk and eaten by the sharks underneath or clubbed and cut into bits and dumped down the gutter drain?"

"Not as many people got clubbed and mugged in the city then statistics say."

"I know. In summers, poor people slept on roofs. But what she's saying and I second to is people have always welled inside them their worst fears and hates and fancies of better futures and love mates till they couldn't fake it anymore and then left like shots out of cannons without telling anyone, not that I see where the welling up part applies to my dad as he battered the crap out of both of us least once a week. As for the bolting from your partner part, maybe women less than men then but maybe now with the changing attitudes changing every week, it's women more than men and who knows if not 3 and 4 times as much to make up for the past 200 years. He had it to here with her she knew and she was in ecstasy when he left and so quietly, though she doesn't see why it had to be on the one night of the year he was always so nice to her. She says the same with Donna too—no camouflaged batterer of course but just someone who couldn't leave her roommate any other way when her fancies or fears welled up in her or only slightly possibly she fell in love with someone else, excuse me, and her pants got so hot and she was so sorry to tell you that she just shot out with this new guy."

"I don't believe any of those. I knew who her lovers were and Donna and I talked things—"

"Look, that's only my mom speaking but in some manner or form I feel too."

"Then what if you help me out this way? Her father might be in a hotel sick or what, as he didn't go back home. So call for him and if the clerk says no Gabe Akers, go this far to ask if any Akers registered there the last 4 days."

"That I think I can do. Hang on, let me get the directory." Picks up another phone. "Hair, health, hobby, hoists, hotels... a to g there's about—"

"This phone being used?" woman asks.

"Hang up and push one of the unlit buttons. A to g about—"

"Don't hog 2 phones, Curt. Listen—just don't."

"I won't, Mrs. Salta. I'm sorry, didn't know it was you."

"That's better." Hangs up.

"See what I got to go through? Think you got a cushy job, great benefits, good salary, perfect hours, not too tiring and plenty of pretty flesh around and time to paint after and what happens but your free and easygoing boss gets caught embezzling the joint and his super straight replacement nails you down every chance she can to prove her integrity and force you to quit so she can stick in her own stooge. One day, and I'm leveling with you honest, when she's blowing her nose I'm going to slip a piece of glass in her coffee. A to g about a hundred of them which is the maxi maxi I could stand calling in one day. I'll try and pawn off the rest of the letters on my mother, whose heart goes way out to you, and my girlfriend and daughter and a couple of our friends same way—Gabe Akers to ask for and if not there, any old Akers over the past 4 days."

"Thanks. And don't do anything with the glass to that woman—it isn't worth it."

"Why not? She runs my ass ragged and is going to cost my job, so let her get hers before."

I call all the airlines in the city and no Akers has booked a flight in 5 days, go to the train station with photos of Donna and foldup traveling frame of her folks she kept on the dresser, am taken into a room below the station where several people are watching surveillance monitors. Each scene on the 40 or so split screens shows a different part of the station: platform, tracks, offices, ticket sellers, waiting area, wash basins and mirrors in the restrooms, corridor leading to here. I show the photos and frame to the security chief and ask if they've seen the young woman or there's been a report on her in the last 4 days and the man since last night.

"Who's this one?"

"Her mother. She died a few years ago. It's only the daughter and father I'm looking for."

"I was going to say. For she looks exactly like the woman who jumped or something in front of an incoming train yesterday and who the police still can't trace, but you say she's already dead—my one's on her last leg. Excuse me," as one of the watchers is pointing to a monitor for him. He looks, presses a knob on a panel board to unsplit the screen, dials the knob to bring the scene closer, talks into a microphone. "Shaney here, station 23C, 23C, I want those kids near Information escorted out of here immediately."

"What're they doing?" voice answers back over a room speaker.

"Ask what they're about to do. You want to wait till they carve someone's elbow off to get her handbag?"

"I didn't want to restrain anyone for only walking through to catch a train or as a shortcut."

"What's he, new here?"

"Laid off rookie cop," someone says. "Flawless record. Commendations galore. Was hired a week ago."

"23C, 23C, this is Shaney speaking, they tell me you're a good man. Well I'm not talking about restraints or arrests, just escort service. They in your picture?"

"Clear, so?"

"Their face and body movements—you telling me they're not here to attack? One in the white flop hat we seized 2 days ago for pursing and handed over to your old force and he's out again, found a home here, dummy wearing the same white hat. It'll take 6 of you to do it." Looks at a train station map on the wall. "16 through 20C go in with you, 22 and 24 as reserves. No arms, but if you have to, clubs."

There's a brief scuffle on the screen between the guards and boys, couple of each knocked down before the boys are walked out of the station. On another monitor we see the boys standing out front, jeering the guards who return to the station and slapping each other's backs and hands, then go over to a man, speak to him, he folds up his newspaper and walks away, they run to him, other side of the monitor picks this up, people around the man and boys watch them, cabs pulling up, discharging passengers, taking on new ones and driving off, city activity, buses and cars passing in the distance, people crossing streets, waiting for lights, man gives the boys some bills from his wallet, they walk away laughing, he looks around, several of the theft's witnesses scatter, he throws his newspaper to the sidewalk, slams his fist into his palm, talks to a passerby who continues to walk, one stops, raises her shoulder, what are we going to do? she seems to say, man walks away, newspaper sheets get blown around, one rises above camera range. Too dark out or just bad reception to catch anyone's expression, but I think I know what the security chief means about the boys' movements.

"Outdoors we don't have jurisdiction," he says to me. "Now what about your friends?"

I give him one of Donna's photos, write out a description of Gabe and promise to have reproductions made of the traveling frame photo so I can send it to him, get written permission to check if any unclaimed luggage has been left in the baggage department in either of their names. I do the same thing at the 2 bus stations, then take the subway and bus to both airports, leave her photos and Gabe's description with the security offices there, check the baggage departments and show Donna's photo to people who work in all the airports' restaurants, bars and smokeshops. A few recognize her as someone they've seen in ads, most say so many people pass through they just remember the most famous.

Curt calls soon after I get home and says "No luck with a to g but had a little extra time and got all the way to j for you. My mom and friends and daughter from her own phone did the rest and all reported back to me and no Akers registered in a hotel since 2 nights ago and just for a couple hours during the afternoon with a much different type woman, but the clerk assumed it was a phony name."

Right after Curt hangs up I get another call. "You were gone a long time."

"Few hours. Who is this?"

"When I dial and dial and get no answer or a busy signal for hours, it always irritates me to no end. This call's important for both of us so I never stopped. You looking for Donna Akers?"

"Know where she is?"

"Just say if it's to be gotten, I think we can get it."

"Who's we?"

"People I represent. We know this neighborhood. Whole city like no one does do we have such good connections, even more than any police organization and maybe all them combined. So if we get her back in one piece alive or only skimpily injured or whatever condition occurred to her by the ones who might have taken her, why care which people find her, isn't that so?"

"I don't know. Sure I want her back, but what do I have to give for all this?"

"You ask 'to give' when someone I hear so close to your life might be at stake?"

"Do, give—what must happen?"

"They'll be a big charge if we find her. We don't, you never again hear from us unless we hear you again might need us, so you've nothing to lose."

"I have no money. Donna does in her savings and coming to her from past jobs which she'll be willing to part with—that is if she is being held against her will and you do get her back."

"If she isn't held against her will, we don't touch her. She is and we find her, then we want the money up front before we turn her over to you."

"I don't know where I could get it if it's a lot."

"It's a lot, what do you think? This could be a big risk so won't be easy. If it's in the neighborhood where you live, it'll be easier so cheaper. Right outside the area, it'll cost more. Way outside or out of the city or state, cost goes up and up because more and more connections have to be made. She's out of the country and being held, it'd cost more than almost anyone has or can get."

"Then I'm sure I won't have enough. I can ask around with friends, but most are poor to average so I doubt they can loan me."

"No. Waste another day, person or people holding her if

they are will have more time to hide her better or further away and then each day's cost to us because of the increased risks and time can go to twice as much till you and your friends will never have enough to pay. You must say now you can pay when we give her to you, since for all we know we might be able to find her in a few hours but then tomorrow till the next week never at all."

"I can't pay."

"Then we'd instead want a favor from you after we get her back if we do."

"What?"

"We'll let you know. Like the money, the favor grows in proportion to how far out of this neighborhood she might be and risks and time we take. Though all our favors are worth a little more in money to us than what you'd pay in cash to get her back, since there's a greater risk, than with someone we're more sure of, in letting an unknown do us the favor."

"What if I don't like the favor asked of me?"

"You can do it all right. We're not that unfair or know nothing about what people can't absolutely do. It won't take much—a few hours to a couple days. We tell you how and when and who or what and what to and you do it, if you consent to that favor now."

"And if I say now I'll do it but later refuse?"

"And we've already got her back for you? To you, to her, that I can't in every detail say. But probably to you both and probably a little more to a lot than what might have happened to her. If nothing did but being taken away and treated fairly okay, than a very lot more to you both and probably by someone or 2 who was in to us for a favor but didn't refuse."

"You sure you can find her?"

"Let me think how I can explain that. You see, we do these sorts of things that might have happened to her and the opposites too, though with her I know we had nothing to do with if anything was—now what do you say?"

"I don't think I can."

"You want her back that much—you can. It's your decision now only and after you say yes you'll hear from us one way or the other, but if you say no you don't hear from us ever again on this matter."

"I'm afraid it's no then."

"No is no then. Goodbye."

"Wait. Maybe for a favor much less you can help me find her father now too."

"No, we're finished for now, Art." Hangs up.

I eat and drink, find another tuna to feed the cat and then clean up its feces on the floor, say "Don't, will you, just don't," try and sleep by drinking some more, finally feel myself falling asleep, cat leaping off, on and off the bed to the window sill till it settles in next to my chest. I dream and wake up sweating, maybe from the heat, it's muggy and hot inside and out and I didn't turn on the air conditioner and forgot the windows were closed, and feel my body for blood and knife holes. Cat's on the sill staring outside, tail in the air like a periscope raised towards me. I usually don't dream much or else don't remember what I've dreamed or at least what I've dreamed by the time I'm a few seconds up. This time some of the dream stays with me. Knife, closet, dumbwaiter, blood, bodies out a window, down a dark hole. Whose blood? What dark hole? Dumbwaiter? Mine? I forget. And an explosion, what kind? I forget. Dream seems very important though. Maybe there's something in it or lots I'm trying to tell myself about Donna that might give me leads where she could be and which didn't come to me in my waking state or else she might be trying to send me something through my dreams or it's just taking place that way without her consciously doing it. I never believed in any sort of thought transference before but now I don't know. Dream: what was it? Knives, doors, closets, holes, window, shove, mob, blood, Donna and I, explosion and noise and almost all those in that order, Donna and I not recognizing the other. I've never been able to pull an unremembered dream out of my head after mulling about it so long after I woke up but this one I'm beginning to. A bedroom: ours. I'm sleeping, Donna comes in the room, gets in bed with me—no, taps my shoulder, I'm in bed alone, it's my bed not hers who is she what's she doing here? I'm thinking in my dream.

Now I know it's Donna but in my dream then I didn't. She's still tapping. I say "What?"

"Where can I hang up my clothes?"

"You've got your own closet. You saying you want mine too, go on, take it, you've already annexed more than half of it," for suddenly I think she lives with me, isn't a stranger, bed I'm in is both of ours.

"What closet?"

"My closet. One on the left."

"Is no left, is no right."

I lift my head over the covers. Closet she regularly uses is a wall. "Then take my child."

"Where's that?"

"Next to where yours used to be."

Opens my closet. It's filled with junk, boots, fishing gear, tv tubes, newspapers piled to the shelf near the top of the closet, which has stacks of photographs on it to the ceiling. She reaches for the light string. "Watch out," I yell. Pulls it, light goes on and everything falls out of the closet. She has to jump out of the way so much stuff falls out. Photographs and newspapers cover the floor and bed I'm in. Her photos, mine, of our parents, friends, us, one of someone I think is my child. A boy. I study it. Now they're all of him, each a different pose and setting and at various ages, from newborn to a boy about 12. "Who's these?" she says.

"Our closet I believe."

"Oh that's droll but how can he be? I've never seen you before."

"Donna."

Puzzled look.

"Donna's your name, come on, and Donna, this is our boy Donald or Don."

"Not a chance. It's your closet Don—I don't live here."

"My son Don. Right. Not a closet and also not something to joke about either." Photo I'm looking at gradually turns from one of the boy to a man somewhat resembling me. "This is ridiculous. It must be a dream. It's too much like a dream.

Things changing preposterously, closet invisibling, your not knowing me."

"What is?"

Then the photo's clearly me. Mustache and beard in the photo gone, full head of hair gone also and nostrils and nose fill out. My teeth, my tongue and gums. I'm back under the covers. Photo: where'd it go? In my hand then gone, magic. I'm snoring in my dream when someone taps my shoulder.

"Where can I dress?"

"Donna?"

"Yes."

"In the room."

"Front of you?"

"You've done it a thousand times before."

"No, not in front of you, not a hundred, not once. I'm modest, I'd feel cheap and small."

"It's dark, my eyes are shut, I'm nearly asleep, I won't see."

"And the closet? It'll see. And the cat? She'll see. The tv. Hat. Jewelry. Coat. Diaries? Tap." Taps my shoulder. I say "Let me snore, let me sleep."

"How can you when there's so much noise."

"Where?"

"Noise I'm talking about. Wake up or get up or turn the dark up but from through there." Room's light. She's pointing to the closet. I hear the noise, like birdcalls, get out of bed, clutch the closet doorknob.

"Should I?"

"What's to be afraid of?" Puzzled look. "Most maybe a cage of them to feed the cats. But you want to, do. Don't want, don't. But one thing, don't do or not it only for me."

"I'll open."

"Why?"

"Might be a water pipe breaking, we could be flooded and drowned. All our things ruined, our neighbors downstairs their apartments ruined too."

"That's bad? That could be good. For us, and serves them. We can get out of here, they can get theirs. But do or don't it's your decision singly, I can swim."

I open it. Man comes stumbling out at me with a knife.
"Swim," I shout.

Many men and women behind him who push me aside to get to her. I shove them back, duck around them, take her hand and run into the next room and shut the door. It's the bathroom I see when I turn the light on. Dumbwaiter's in the bathroom under the window when it isn't either in real life. People pounding on the door. "Come out," they say. "Now, come out, you both, quick, to get yours."

"Go down the dumbwaiter," I tell her.

I press my shoulder and foot against the door when they start forcing it open.

"The dumbwaiter goddamnit," I shout when I see her naked in front of the medicine chest mirror putting on lipstick.

"I'll get filthy."

"You'll get killed and tortured, sodomized and worse. Cowed, teased, browbeaten, maligned." I grab the lipstick from her and then the hair dryer when she turns that on and starts blowing her hair and throw them in the dumbwaiter. "Follow them."

Door's forced open a little, I force it closed. Open, closed. Opened even more. A lock's on the door and bolt right above it. How could I've not seen and used them, known they were there? I try to force the door closed to lock and bolt it but they force it open all the way and drag the broken door into the hall. About 15 of them, too many to fit in the room at once. Knives, in the air and one slashing at me, big and little knives, some a foot long and curved, most half that size and straight. I take the knife from the lead attacker by twisting her wrist and catching the knife as it drops. She reaches for a hilt in her belt sheath. I stick the knife in her belly, step back to avoid her falling and guts spilling out but nothing but a little blood does. Donna's trying to fit head first into the dumbwaiter which now looks more like an incinerator and has a flap instead of a door. I fight the other knifers off with the knife I took from the woman's sheath and with my free hand push Donna's rear end further into the incinerator. Her feet get in and drop and I hear her shriek and then a thud from below. I'm slashed on the arm by someone when I'm opening the incinerator flap to look inside and blood spouts out of the cut but I don't feel weakened or hurt. "You son of, now look what you've done, are making me do." I stick the knife in his belly. He falls on the woman. I grab the bandanna off his forehead and wrap it around my cut, take the knife from his hand and one from inside his belt and fight 2 of them at once, slashing and sticking the knife in their bellies. I leave these knives in and take the ones from their hands and another from one of their sheaths so I can fight 3 of them at once, 2 with 2 knives in my right hand. I slash and jab, 3 people drop. I take their knives and 2 from their sheaths and fight 5 of them into the hallway. There are about 30 on each side of me out there, maybe a hundred down the hallway into the livingroom, all with knives in their hands, or between their teeth, inside their belts, in sheaths around their waists and calves and thighs, little knives over their ears, littler ones poking through their nostrils and ear lobes, on chains around their necks, in their hair as barrettes, several of them with knives in bandoliers crossing their chests. I get back to the bathroom, stack the dead and twitching bodies to block the door entrance, squeeze into the incinerator and dive down the chute. It's a long dark drop. She's on her knees at the bottom of it, arms outstretched to me, shaking her head, shouting "Don't, Art, jump," blood on her face I see as I get nearer, one of her breasts badly cut, hole in her stomach dribbling out white grease, cheek slit, lips sliced, stitches on her forehead, bandaged hands, punctured arms. She covers her eyes, my head dives right into hers and our skulls crack. Atoms split and begin to bounce in our joined brains and then it's black with sporadic flashing light and all I can see in this light which lasts less than a second each is her uninjured nose and shimmery perfect teeth and feel her hands I think they are stroking my cheeks and dream ends.

I have all this written down and study it. "Cats" she mentioned in the dream could be the one sleeping on the bed and missing leopard coat but what's it mean? Knives: phallic and real fear perhaps but going past that meaning what? Her punctured arms: do I suspect she took needled drugs when I had no overt thought about it before? I don't know but don't think so but it could be a lead, but all that's probably just fearing the worst for her again along with those cuts and holes and bandaged hands and mob and her being nude through all this. The closet? Fear again and if so of what? Remembrance from when I was in the womb? Fear of the eventual tomb? Mine? Donna's? All that might be mildly interesting another time though more likely insipid and routine, and now none of it helps. The boy—his both being in the photos and alluded to as my son and a closet. Both of us wanted a child, boy or girl, me sooner than she, I had no preference which sex, she preferred a girl because as she said "What would I do with a boy if we split up and I kept it?" but that's not what I'm looking for now. Maybe it's her diary child and marriage and what she actually felt about our relationship that she's hidden in the closet from me, which sure, makes me doubt her somewhat and maybe even changes my feeling for her a little, but how does all that help me figure out anything here? Things get hidden in closets, hung up, thrown on the floor, stored for years or lost. As a boy I used to hide in closets, but all kids did. I don't recall but I'm sure Donna told me she hid in one as a child too. I went to movies then which frequently had closets with trap doors or secret passages leading to danger and freedom through them and particularly slapsticks and cheap mysteries and swashbuckling films. There's the old expression "to come out of the closet." Do I think I have to come out of one and if so from what? Also the water closet which could be why I said the pipe might be breaking, but what did it mean when I added "we could be flooded and drowned"? Filled closet spilling out? Oldtime radio and tv shows had those and maybe the new ones too, but in my dream it might've been a catchall for our domestic troubles, years we've lived together, mess she could be in now, with the fishing gear meaning someone searching for things under water or search of any kind including for symbols but especially to recover tools or other equipment down a drilled well or just a futile expedition on my part to fish whatever I can out of the sea. She called the cat a she. Does she know? Maybe it was the one extrasensory wave out of many to make it to me from her. I pick up the cat and keep parting its hair down there while it claws at me to be released and hisses and I think cries and nicks my fingers and wrist and this time see it's a he with its scrotum cut off. I set him down on the bed, he jumps off and runs away. "Closet invisibling" I said. "What's to be afraid of?" and "Don't, Art, jump" she said. Lock and bolt on the door when I should've seen them right off. Each of these and really any of the rest of it could be interpreted many ways, though Donna, an amateur dream genius she once called herself with a bookshelf devoted to them, said no dream can be interpreted obviously, though that I don't know now too. Read and heard plenty of other people's dream theories and they go all ways.

Phone. Let it while I try to interpret further but pick it up. "This the Akers place?" woman says.

"Akers and Alimin both."

"We've only an Akers here—Gabe M. Could you come get him? He doesn't seem well."

"This a hospital?"

"No, but we wanted to have them come or ourselves take him to one but then thought for all of us best not. We're called Arcadia Club 2, East 31st number 8. They've 3 other Arcadias near here, number 3 east on 31st some more, so don't get us mixed up. Number 8. You'll recognize us by the big yellow banner with our logo outside on the pole—I'll make sure to keep the light on it. We close at 4 so get here sooner as he has to be out by then and it might take some doing getting him downstairs. Ask for the manager Elly. I'm busy, wait."

Cab over, long flight up. Booth with woman in 2 piece bathingsuit behind it who says "Good evening, sir, little late but like to sign here and join our club? Won't have much browsing time but I think enough."

"Elly?"

"Me? No, nothing alike, but you who I'm to be on the lookout for the old man? She's tied up now but take a seat and she'll meet you. That'll be 15 dollars club membership plus 1.20 tax."

"Elly said nothing about money. I don't have any—cab fare finished me. You know where the man is?"

"Sleeping in back still. You have no money? One thing I know is nobody gets in or can even loiter in this alcove for more than 30 seconds without paying."

"I don't want to do anything but pick up my father-in-law."

"Sure, fine, pick him up, drop him a few times, yank him out by his hair, whatever. But once you're in there, how do the girls know?"

Man in the checkroom comes over. "You don't have the money you fly right downstairs, monkey, or I fly you down first."

"I don't want a girl. I'm here to get the man who's apparently sick back there."

"The old one? You dumb, Cam? He's here to get him off our back. Let him in."

"I was told never to let anyone in who didn't pay the fee. Mrs. so and so gets wind you let one in and I let him go through too, we'll both be in a sling, long as you been here, Swank."

"I know it's okay. This man of his is sick."

"Right, but your neck not mine, remember that. You'll put it down in writing for me?"

"I put nothing down in writing."

"Put it down or I don't buzz him in. Now down. On paper. That you take full charge letting this man in free with no tax."

"Give me a paper and pen."

"Where'm I getting paper? Why should I supply everything?"

"Tear it out of the back of the guestbook."

"Mrs. so and so sees her precious guestbook wrecked, we'll get bounced just for that too."

Swank searches his pockets and comes up with a flyer for the club—*15 Girls, Women, Girls! Satisfaction Guaranteed or Money Back! From All Exotic Lands! In Every Tongue! Beautiful Girls, Women, Girls, Only!*—slaps it facedown on the guest book which has a column of names on it, John this, Jim that, just John or Jim, names of movie, tv and sports stars and presidents of the country past, present and ancient and the mayor and governor's names and several other wellknowns plus a few that look fake: Stick E. Glue. Frank Lee Perverse, and writes *I take responsibility (full) for this man*—"What's your name?"

"Art Alimin."

Art Alleyman going in for old man in back his sick farther with no charge (room D) tax too. Looks at watch. *3:45 a.m. Swank.* Gives it to her, door opens. I go in.

"If I see Elly before you I'll tell her," Cam says. "Meanwhile, sit but no tricks."

Benches are against all 4 walls and I sit on one. 3 men on the other 3 benches. 2 women, one in underwear and other in boxing shorts and sequined t-shirt with I guess her name on it, Tough Tess, play a board game on the floor, portable radio on the table next to them with lively dance music on. Third woman's reading on the bench I'm on, feet and knees up, massaging and picking between her toes. Good novel. Read it or almost finished it when I had to return it to the library because it was overdue. Her lips move as she reads. Switches feet, looks at me, down at the book. Up down several times with an expression maybe she knows me, then about anything but the book could she care less. A man stands, stretches, starts for the woman on the bench—she tucks her heels into her buttocks further—swivels around, heads for the door, stops, snaps his fingers, turns to the players—both look up at him, smile, go back to the game—and taps Tess on the head. She stands, rubs her head where he tapped it, takes his ticket and says "This way." They go through the door I came in.

"Ranier, you want to take over for Tess? I can't play by myself."

Reading woman doesn't answer.

"Ranier, want to or not? You're ahead if you do. She was slaughtering me."

Doesn't say, turns page, untucks her heels and kneads big toe.

"You want to play sir?" to me. "She thinks she's smart and deaf when she's no. —You're no. Only joking with her. She knows we're friends."

"I don't know how."

"Easy, I'll teach. We each get 5 pieces, a team-planner, safecracker, gunman, the rest—and you roll the dice and move your team so many boxes closer underground to the bank you want to rob. But a bad throw could mean your team getting picked off one by one by marksmen cops or natural disasters or their own mistakes like their explosives blowing up or sewer overflowing or one card even where a robber gets bitten to death by sewer pipe rats. If you get just one person through the floor other than the strongarm with the winning combination throws and no alarms off and the bank guard sleeping and getaway car starting and all the road to your waiting helicopter clear, you break the safe and fly to a tropical isle free as can be with 14 million cash and because of your political connections in both countries, no extradition permitted for life."

"Sounds like fun but I'm waiting for Elly. She might only be another minute and then you'll have to get someone else."

"Any you fellows?"

One man shakes his head, other puts on sunglasses, turns up his jacket collar.

"I hate late hour. I'll be glad when I get home and eat if there was only some tv on that hour. Hey, wake up, what's with you guys, just here to look? Place closes in half an hour. I haven't made my quota. I got mouths to feed, in-laws to support, watchdogs that cost more to feed than us all together. You got back troubles, ulcers, I'll make you well. Give you the soothingest feeling rubdown of your life."

"Yeah, back problems, ulcers both," man without glasses says. "Make me well."

"Hurray, I've a live one." Gets up, man too. "Anybody not mind the radio? Ranier? Sunglasses? You're all angels. You 2 fellows want to take over the game? He can teach you," she says to him.

"No thanks," I say.

"Good. It's my game anyway and I don't want any of the pieces lost. Lose one important one, like the helicopter, and it wouldn't seem the same." Folds the game into its box, goes with the man and radio down the hall.

"It's dead here without music," Ranier says to me.

"How long you think Elly will be?"

"You want Elly, you should have Elly. She's a very nice person."

"She phoned me for the sick man somewhere in here—know anything about him?"

"Only that I hope he's okay. Last time Elly looked she said he was. He was talking to us right on this bench. First we felt he could sleep off whatever it is we thought he had. Then when he looked worse, she thought we'd wait till he awaked and persuade him to a hospital. Elly's in charge here this week so I listened to her, though I had other ideas."

"How'd he get up here?"

"From downstairs, when he walked past, our card man on the street stopped him and said 'Looking for anything special?' He said for his daughter and our man said 'I'm sure she's upstairs,' because he thought your old man was using the daughter as a metaphor for the same thing he was trying to interest him in and he gets a cut of and sent him up to us. So your old man paid his dues and looked around but didn't seem surprised not to see his daughter and sat between Elly and me while I'm thinking oh my god, you're taking a big chance taking on someone old as him, and looked disconsolate and spoke incoherent is the best way I can put it—jumbo jump talk about his daughter, hunting a day for her, because the city's at best a small ineffectual snare when you get right down to it he said. Then when he's explaining what he meant about that snare phrase, which I asked him to just to make talk until someone else chose me so I wouldn't have to go in with him, he collapsed across Elly's lap. 'All we need now,' she screamed as she already had to deal with a guy who tried to tie a wire around our youngest girl's neck who he mistook for his sister 30 years ago because she stole his seed and warped him then, focus on that. We took your old man into a room to sleep it off, thinking him drunk or something though there was no sign on his breath. When he continued sleeping and so restlessly, I felt we should get him to a hospital but she thought it less damaging for everyone including him if he woke up and went to one himself."

The man sits next to me, takes off his glasses, cleans them, turns his collar down. "What this beautiful young lady says is the truth. I was here."

"Thanks but I hardly need a backup. A few hours later when we still couldn't rouse him, Elly phoned Mrs. so and so and got her assistant who said look for his wallet and call someone he knows in it but get him out fast. You find no one, he said, put him in a taxi with his money to his home address and if no cabby will deliver him or he lives too far for a cab ride out of town, leave him on the street. She found his next of kin on an i.d. For a while she didn't want to call thinking she could be his wife or someone close or once close like that, a sister or niece at the least, since we knew his home address was upstate. Now Elly thinks it was dumb not to have taken him to a hospital right away and signed him in to emergency and just left him there, and if she hadn't gotten hold of you she would've done that rather than calling an ambulance or leaving him on the next street."

"Do you know what illnesses could be wrong with him?" man asks me.

"No, but he is pretty old so it could be anything—his heart."

"You're not his son then?"

"No."

"Because your concern, I thought you were. Then that's very nice."

"I'd say heat or heart too," Ranier says. "I was once almost a grade teacher and we learned first aid, so I did what I could till I couldn't with him anymore because I either forgot or that's where our medical training stopped and since kids didn't get coronaries that much, not to be flippant, they probably didn't teach me about that. For the prostration it was always the lie back, open the collar, wet rag and massaging the hands which I did. But he'll be all right."

"Why do you say that?"

"Because I do, that's all."

"She's also a smart beautiful girl so if she thinks it, take her advice."

"Would you take me to his room now," I say to her.

"Please wait for Elly. She should've been out by now."

"But maybe I can help him and quicker we get him to the hospital the better."

"Just wait, don't cause trouble," man says. "Not so much with me, I'm only a guest. But the lobby guy—he's scrawny but a mean sonofagun. Card man's even crazier but he's gone for the day. But Swank, he can get tippy like almost no man I've seen can. What he did to that creep with the wire scared even me."

Couple come into the room from the hallway, she squeezing his elbow. "You'll be here next Monday?" he says.

"Saturday's my last. They move us around every week."

"Where'll you be—I'll come see you."

"We never know. Doesn't have to be one of the Arcadias. Phone here and ask Swank where Elly is this week. By that time I'll phone him to say where." They shake hands and he leaves.

"El," Ranier says, "this is the man for the old man."

"Glad you got here. I think he's okay. He was breathing easier last I looked in on him, even opened his eyes and seemed to know me."

"If I told you I was a doctor," man in sunglasses says, "would you be very mad?"

"You're not a doctor," Elly says.

"No, but I only wanted to know what your reaction would be. Now I know."

Elly and I go down the hall and into a room. Gabe's on the bed. Shoes off, tie loosened, rag on his head. I take it off. It's cold. Hold his hand. That's cold. Put my ear to his chest. No sound. Ear to his mouth: no breath. Cheeks cold, body's cold, hands swollen, fingers ballooned. I take off his socks. Feet cold. Rub them. They stay cold. Chest for beat, wrist for pulse, mouth for breath. Back and forth, chest wrist mouth, beat pulse breath, trying to get a sign on him, some life. "Call an ambulance and get Ranier in."

"What's she to do?"

"Just get her in, don't argue, and the ambulance."

"Maybe the ambulance but why Ranier?"

"She said she was once almost a teacher and learned first aid."

"She's full of it. They're all full of it out there. I'm the only one here who isn't so talk to me, you think he's dead?"

"Yes."

"So what's an ambulance going to do or Ranier?" Puts her ear to his chest and mouth. "I got a mirror. I'll check his breath with it."

"They only do that in movies."

"You can do it in life too. Where you think they got the idea from?" Runs out of the room, I try and take his pulse, feel his temples, comes back with her pocketbook, Ranier and the man behind her—"Get out of here you 2," slams door—takes the mirror out and sticks it against his lips. "Not a breath. Nothing on him. I think he's dead too. Now we're in trouble. I am. You maybe too. His people won't want it to be known he died here and Mrs. so and so will who knows what she'll do if she finds out and her boss. First time when I'm acting manager, a little more pay, I don't take her assistant's instructions what to do, oh what a fool."

"What he do, just fall over on you?"

"Yes. Just fell over. We were talking. Leave me alone. I said before he was breathing to me just before, recognized me. Forget about that. What are we going to do? Now I'm up a creek. Forget the extra pay, they told me to get him out of here quick, put him on the street, even if he's sleeping or very sick if there was no other way like he can go there himself and that's what we should've done. Me."

"Let me try some things first. Ask anyone out there if they know about resuscitation."

"Nobody does."

"Ask."

"But nobody does. I know them. Ranier and I travel together from place to place. She knows books, she knows hair. The crazy in the coatroom, his breathing into anyone's mouth would kill them instead of revive."

"He might've been in the army—a medic."

"Never."

"Ask the man in sunglasses."

"He's crazy."

"Maybe he is a doctor. Something about the way he said it seemed as if same time he was denying it he was trying to make you believe it."

"He's a bullshit artist. He's crazy. He wouldn't touch this man's hand if he knew it could bring him to life. He stays here all day looking, feeling himself."

"Then one of the other women and customers."

"No." I start for the door. "You bother one of them, say

anything, I'll get Swank and he'll bring his switch on you. Now what are we going to do? Think."

I give mouth to mouth resuscitation. Come up: "Call an ambulance."

"No and don't bug me about it. No. No."

"They might have some equipment to get him back."

"They have nothing. You can't get him back. Out for so long, you think his brains will be worth preserving? For a jar? He's dead. I've read about these things. Stop that," while I'm giving mouth to mouth. "It won't work. What are we going to do? Fucking creek. In the office they learn I let him die, I can get stumped. Things are bad enough with them with the city. They want to lay low. They don't want a scandal going. Is he someone important?"

Up: "No. Modest man. Little money. Give me more time."

"Make it quick. They come around 4:30 latest to pick up their receipts and check the rooms to see nobody's sleeping overnight and lock up and I don't want them seeing him. Girls won't talk and Swank can be bought. Look," while I'm giving mouth to mouth, "I was good enough to call you or your lady even if a little too late maybe, way too late. But I was good enough to and the old man I didn't throw out. I talked nice to him, made him feel comfortable. He never should've been let in but nobody gets stopped but punk kids and crazy drunks. Okay, I didn't throw him out when I could've, when I should've, put him on the street, let him lay there and pass away if that's what was going to happen, like any smarter place would. He was going to die anyway tonight, any stairs would've killed him, it wasn't anything we did or fault here, so think of something to help me now, please."

Pound his chest. Seen it done in the next bed when my mother was a patient once. I sit on top of Gabe and push my palms down on his chest and then pound it twice with my hand clasped around my fist and push down and pound again twice and do these 2 a few more times and lean over him and breathe into his mouth and push and pound and breathe and again and again these 3 and fall exhausted on him and again those 3 but he's dead.

I climb off. But I'm no doc so how can I be sure he's dead? I put my ear to his mouth and chest, feel his hands and feet and lips and cheeks and nose and toes. They're all cold, eyelids have opened, fingers more swollen, now his forearms too and they're wet and turned a little blue.

"Enough?"

"I'll walk him out and you call an ambulance to meet me downstairs."

"Great. I'll help you to the door. Thanks. Swank will help you down the stairs. There's a phonebooth at the corner a few steps away. If you don't mind, because there's a real shortage of time, and I just think it best if anyone's looking or if they say where'd you call from to call from there."

We put Gabe's shoes and socks on him, straighten his tie, leave his shirt open, put his hat on, stand him up, hat falls off.

"Forget the hat. Throw it away."

Squashes and sticks it in his back pocket, won't fit, sticks it in mine, takes one side, I the other, "Wait," she says, "sit him down first." We sit him on the bed and I sit beside him holding him up. She opens the door. "Swank, come here please," she yells. "You," she says to the man in sunglasses who was at the door with Ranier when Elly opened it, "We're all through, goodnight."

"Goodnight. —Goodnight" to me and he leaves.

"Ranier, knock on the rest and tell them very unexcitedly to stay in there with their friends till I—"

"They've all gone."

Swank and I carry Gabe downstairs and stand him up on the landing. Elly says from the top steps. "Thanks mister. You really helped out. You need me for anything, well what could you? but I'll be here or other places, and look around good before you hit the street."

Swank leaves me at the door holding onto Gabe and goes outside. "Okay, no one," and we walk Gabe to the car next to the phonebooth, lean him against the fender and Swank says "Got him?" and I say yes and he goes back to the building. Nobody's around, no cars. Mostly a business district. All the building windows are dark. I turn him over and lie him partly across the hood. Billfold shows in back. Maybe something in it about

Donna that could help. Pictures of her and her mother. His mother in early to midcentury dress. Both mothers and Gabe and Donna when she was a girl all posing as their town's original settlers on Settlement Day. Donna has the same snaps. Bus ticket back. Stamps. Cards. Licenses. Money, not much. I take it except for a couple dollars and stick the billfold back. Car pulls up and parks in front of the Arcadia, 2 men get out, look at me standing beside Gabe and go inside. Isn't stealing. I need it to look for his daughter. Maybe it is legally stealing but so what? He'd want me to. Maybe he wouldn't but so what? If the money's needed to send him upstate to be buried I'll use it, I swear. Other pockets are filled with newspaper and magazine clippings of Donna and new and used tissues and other paper scraps.

I call hospital emergency and say "A friend of mine seems to have had a heart attack on the street and might be dying, I don't know." Man says he'll send an ambulance over and that I should call the police to come too.

They come. Doctor says Gabe's dead. Ranier and Swank and Elly leave the building and walk the other way. The men leave right after them and drive off. I go to the hospital with Gabe and a policeman who asks what happened.

"We were both looking for his daughter. About—"

"Wait a—what do you mean his daughter?"

"She's been missing or just walked away but for more than 4 days. It's a long story. The 15th precinct knows and I'll tell you after but let me get through with this first for your report while it's still fresh in my head. About a half hour ago," and I look at Gabe and say "Can't we do this when we get him to the hospital?" and at the hospital after they wheel Gabe away I say "Mr. Akers called me almost an hour ago from that phonebooth where you found us at, or maybe from another one on the same avenue and street because once I saw him by one I didn't look around anywhere else. He said he wasn't feeling well and could I come to pick him up. I cabbed right over and when I got there found him leaning against the car. He couldn't speak, just kept pointing to his chest and mouth like he couldn't get his breath and his eyes were popping out and when I tried to sit him he caved in on me with his incredible weight and so fast that before I could stop him he fell."

"I know what you mean."

"Right?—incredibly heavy and fast. I turned him over so he could lie on the hood and not fall and called the hospital and police and after I got back to him from the booth he seemed to be dead. I tried mouth to mouth breathing and even pounding his chest which might be the reason he has bruises there if they happen to find them but nothing worked."

"You did what you could I guess."

"I tried, I breathed, I massaged, I pounded, I tried."

"Easy, it's what I said, I know."

Hospital doctor tells me that anybody who dies on a public street has to be autopsied by the city medical examiner. "They're picking him up now but asked if you know of a relative or guardian to see to him after."

"Just a daughter who disappeared 4 days ago and nobody knows where she is. Besides her, not even a distant cousin on either side—his or hers, they've both told me that."

"Then he'll be put on ice for a week after the postmortem and if no relative shows, they'll get a legal official from his town to tell them what they want done with him. No relative turns up or refuses to have anything to do with it, the city as a courtesy to us removes what they still can from the body that can be put to some future medical use and sends these parts to the hospital the body was taken from. With his age and time he'll be on ice and their antiquated cooking system, I doubt they'll be much we can use."

2 detectives come, policeman gives them a copy of his report and goes. They ask me questions, phone the 15th precinct to check my story about Donna, one says "An artist across the street from the phonebooth before said he saw you turning the old man over and going through his pockets but not pounding his chest or breathing into him and things like you say on here. He even called the police on you thinking it was a mugging but the patrol car got there after the ambulance and police you called had left."

"He's a liar, that's all there is to it, or doesn't see well or maybe didn't wear his glasses or had on the wrong prescription, for I pounded on his chest and breathed into him on and off and all sorts of restorative devices and didn't go through his wallet."

"Who said wallet? Pockets."

"Wallets, pockets, that's what he's inferring, that I was stealing, looking for something to steal—from a billfold, wallet, changepurse, moneyclip, coinpocket, anything, you name it—watch and ring."

"We ask you: why would he? His was the absolute good samaritan act—he had too much to lose. Loft he lives in is illegal, kerosene stove by city law he's also not allowed to own, smell of dope when the investigating officers walked in and what looked like a 12 year old with no top on in his bed, when he's around 55. Now why?"

"Maybe he's smoked too much and his brains went or the kerosene fumes or paint remover got to them sooner. All I know and can never forget is how I pounded and breathed till I nearly dropped and that his mouth smelled from peppermint, I remember, peppermint."

Checks a sheet. "Half used roll of minted antacids was found in his shirt pocket."

"There, okay, for how'd I know?"

"Could've found them when you were frisking his pockets if what the artist says is true. But massaging his feet it says here. You took off his shoes and socks to do it and then put them back on and tied them?"

"Only the ankles and fingers, no feet, and very briefly—rubbed them with both hands like this. I tried to untie his shoelaces but they or just me couldn't get them untied—too flustered or they weren't loops but knots. Maybe that's what your artist saw—my massaging and stuff, trying to pry his tight shoes off, which he took for my going through his pockets. Anyway, it's his word and his girlfriend's against mine, from across the street—"

"We have she didn't see anything. Was too asleep at the time. Doesn't want to get her name down, probably a runaway, which makes his story more plausible for what he might have to lose, harboring her, though we're not saying he saw exactly right."

"The only he from across the street, nighttime, 4 to 5 o'clock, who knows how dirty his windows or far away I was from the streetlight. But you have to understand. Mr. Akers was the father of the woman I've lived like husband to her wife with for 3 years. I loved him, love her. I wouldn't do anything like steal his money. He was a dear charming guy and was always incredibly generous to me."

"Like how?"

"Like saying nice things, not dumping on me to her, nothing by way of money I meant, and I wouldn't take a pencil off Gabe, one of those mint pills."

"We're only repeating what a witness said, not saying he couldn't've misread what he honestly thinks he saw. I'm sure if you told him what you did by the phonebooth he'd go along with you that he was wrong. Though don't let what I say goad you like you have to get hold of him to change his mind."

"Why should I? I'm grateful to him—he stepped in in his way. Other people, they'd let the blinds drop, hide. He did what he thought was right and besides I'm a peaceful guy. But now I only want to get home. I'm worn out. Then I want to see after a long sleep what I can still do to find Gabe's daughter."

"We want you, we'll call or come by."

On the way out I pass the hospital's chapel, stop in to sit and rest. Porter wakes me. "Thought of doing it an hour ago but you seemed too beat and not like a bum off the street. Now I've got to lock up for 20 minutes to sweep around here and wax your seat because visitors begin coming in to pray before the operations about now."

I go home, toss Gabe's hat towards the chair, cat catches it in midair, plays with it, bites the band and feather off, claws the feather to shreds and eats them, coughs it up, takes the hat behind the couch and leaves it there. I clean up the mess, with Gabe's money buy food for myself and the cat and a flea collar as I'm beginning to itch from what look like flea bites, and a bag of kitty litter and toy mouse with a bell in it which I throw to him. He goes into an attacking stance from a few feet off, pounces on it, sniffs and kicks it, runs behind the couch and starts tearing up the rest of the hat.

By phone I place an ad in the public notices of all the city newspapers saying "Attention, please, Attention! Anyone knowing anything about the whereabouts or disappearance of Donna Akers, 16 East 12th Street, last seen leaving the Coliseum movie theater here last Thursday night around 11 p.m., please contact Art Alimin, same address, 324-1279, anytime, day or night, or through this personal notices section. Please: no eccentrics and crank callers or correspondents need apply. Complete secrecy and privacy sanctified. If required reward will be provided though realize I'm not by a long shot even a moderately prosperous person besides being unemployed and that whatever property and savings Miss Akers and her recently deceased father Gabe might have I can't in any way acquire. Thank you."

Each ad taker phones back to confirm the notice and the last one says "Excuse me but the use of the words 'night' and 'p.m.' is redundant in the grouping beginning with 'last seen leaving the Coliseum movie theater.' Remove night and you'll save, with just that one additional printing space, the cost of a line of copy, while with p.m. you won't."

"Read it to me over in full please?" and she does and I say "Take out night but only because the notice makes more sense that way."

I call Donald and get him at home.

"You sonofabitch," he says. "It's all your fault. Why'd you ever tell him? I'll never forgive you for this but for now don't let those butchers cleave a piece of any part off or out of him, you hear? Forget it—you'll botch that too. I'm flying down and claiming I'm Gabe's nephew and will have the authorized forged papers to prove it and taking him back and seeing he gets a decent funeral and burial in the Akers graveyard. You come to it and I and a dozen of his friends will bury you too, though not there."

"I have to come."

"Do and what I said will be the truth, Art. You'll get tarred, feathered, forever missing and dead. It's been done before around here. Probably nobody's been so dumb to drop a single hint about it till now. And tell anyone anything I just mentioned and I hear of it and you'll get buried by me personally for that too."

"I'm sure you're not serious about any of this but I'll accept what you said as if you are."

I go through each room. Look under every couch seat and rug. In all the drawers, cabinets and shelves. Through her footwear and clothes. Behind mirrors and picture frames. Turn her family desk upsidedown for a possible button or latch to a hidden compartment. Read all the letters she's saved. Find the one diary the police left behind which was begun by her mother day Donna was born and continued by Donna 4 years later. Rummage through her modeling portfolios, personal folders and all our books. Look inside the laundry hamper and storage containers and jars and under plants and stacks of dishes and pots. Cut open our mattress in several places and probe inside. Rip the linings out of her suitcases and handbags. Everything. Empty coffee cans under the sink. Dump the plants over and squeeze the dirt. Loose tea. Tap all the floorboards to see if any are loose or hollow underneath. Feel inside the back cleft of the bathroom sink pedestal. Unclasp the mirror and picture frames and check behind the cardboard. Pull the refrigerator out. Get on my knees and feel behind the stove for anything that might have been dropped or stored there and a cockroach runs out. I jump back. It plays dead. When I look around for something to swat it with it starts up the wall. "Goddamnit," I scream and swing at it and my hand goes through the wall under the sink. Didn't know it was just thin plaster but thought it solid brick. Now I've a hole the size of a softball. Space behind the hole is about a foot deep and seems to run the entire length and height of the wall. Pipes are inside. Decayed newspapers. I want to look at the top one but don't want to touch. Other things I can't reach. I poke the hole larger till I can get my head and a lamp inside. Old magazines and pieces of rotting cloth and bottles and sink parts and lines of floor and wall paneling and tree limbs and a tiny animal's bones and books and dust. I grab a newspaper, shake it inside the hole and take it out. It's written in another language and is about 40 years old. War Declared! I think it says or something close, like Battle Rages! or Nation Invaded! for the photo underneath shows hundreds of foot soldiers and a few horsemen, surrounded by smoke and craters from explosions, charging through barbed wire. But who knows what will be running through the hole if I don't close it up. I try masking tape. Wall's damp and tape keeps peeling off. I try holding down the masking tape with cellophane tape but neither stick. I bang the floor again and again with my fists. Linoleum underneath feels loose. I tear it up and continue tearing up a couple square feet of it till the joined linoleum won't come undone.

I go outside and buy plaster and place in the wall newspapers and magazines and books and accumulated supermarket bags and old clothes and broken pots and much of the junk I just made out of her suitcases and handbags and mattress stuffing and wall plaster chips and linoleum strips and break 2 dilapidated chairs and pile that in with jars of pebbles and shells from past vacations we took till they cover and just about fill in the hole space. I mix and smear plaster on that and when it dries more plaster mix to the hardened part till the hole's patched and then flatten it out to the rest of the wall. I resume looking through the apartment for anything that might explain Donna being gone or give me a new clue where to look for her but find there's no other place to look. Toilet tank, and I run into the bathroom and lift the cover but nothing's inside but equipment and water. Except for what the detectives read to me from her diaries they have, there's little in any of what I found or read today that I didn't know before other than for things like her summer growing spurt of 7 inches when she was 13, time she defecated in a bathtub when she was 8 to avenge her parents who left her home and her babysitter as a lesson to her mashed it in her face, her first soul kiss though she didn't know what it was called then when she was 10, hour, minute and date she first observed she had a "dictator's mustache of hair down there," how she felt when she first masturbated—"Like they say, not all it's cracked up to be, yuk yuk, and oh you kid, though maybe I rubbed it the wrong way," name of the boy who first touched "not my chocolate bits, which I wouldn't permit, but the little raised skin around it that I presumptuously call my tits," foods she loathed as a girl, competitive school games she hated to play because she didn't like to shove or be shoved or toss a dodgeball at anyone or even compete, horses she could feed, curry and hug all day, first time she menstruated, successfully parked a car, piloted a motorcycle, skydived and mountain climbed, found a hairstyle she liked, whimsically stole a slip, also newspaper photos of her being escorted by the young king of pickled fish, queens of fashion, merchant princes, supperclub jesters, gossip columns and people in the news pieces about her alleged romances with this pop star, that movie luminary, socialites, media brights, moguls, notables, solons, but 4 to 5 years ago at the latest and for me nothing usable or really new.

I clean the apartment, put on the street the mattress and rest of the mess I didn't seal behind the wall, call Bo the detective who seemed to be in charge of Donna's case and say "I don't know if you know it or not but Miss Akers is still missing."

"I'm sorry."

"But what the hell's being done about it damnit?"

"Don't give me that tough shit."

"Then what's being done about it then if I can ask?"

"You got something new to give me on it?"

"No."

"So?"

"Can I get her diaries back at least?"

"Why not? Go to Properties here in the basement and see Sergeant Lux."

I go to Properties. Sergeant Lux unlocks a cage, goes in, looks around, scratches his head, blows his nose, snaps his fingers and smiles to himself, unlocks a walk-in safe inside the cage and goes in, "Oh, could you slam the cage door till it snaps locked please?" he yells to me, I see him walking back and forth past the safe door several times, puts a cigarette in his mouth though a freshly lit one hangs off the edge of his desk, throws the match to the floor when it burns his fingertips, lights the cigarette with another match, locks the safe and says through the cage "Strange, but it's not in either storage place I thought I put it in."

"What do you mean it? There are diaries and letters."

"Right, them, but neither's in either room. If they were drugs or cash I'd say someone could have taken it. But they were just paper, sentimental value only, unless she wrote things someone didn't want read. We do have rats in the basement and cats to keep the rat birthrate down. But the rats get so big they chase away the cats in packs, and if the diaries were bound by old-fashioned glue, the rats could have eaten them, but I don't see how they could have eaten them all—glue, pages, covers too if they weren't real leather. Even so, they couldn't devour them all and letters too in 2 days. I'll find them and give you a call." Takes my number. "I don't, well, put in a missing claims. Minimum, you'll get from the city the going rate for what leatherbound diaries sell for today, though I doubt anything for the letters."

I go back to Bo and say "I think I do have something new on where Donna might be."

"Yeah, where's that?"

"Not actually where but the man who might've abducted her—it's the best I've got."

"No, give it, some of our biggest pigs have been caught and put away by the littlest tips."

"From a panhandler admittedly—"

"Oh, a panhandler."

"He seemed more than that and said he saw the man who burglarized our apartment—carrying the stolen things only minutes after. Can I give you a description of the man?"

"Panhandler or supposed burglar?"

"Why would you want the panhandler's?"

"Why the supposed burglar?"

"He probably burglarized for one thing. And might be the same man, because nobody else found how he could've gotten in, who kidnapped Donna."

"You want burglaries, go to room 210, which is Thefts. You want to reopen her case, give me something substantial, not a half dead bag of rags left overnight on the street."

"He wasn't so bad off. Shabby and weird acting perhaps, but he even said he has a phone number where to reach him, not that I should believe him."

"You have it? Let me see. 'Erratic?' That's a number? What's he use when you want to reach him long distance, 'loose screwball'? But this I have to call."

"Forget it."

"No, it's this week's must." Starts dialing.

"He said he might not be in—that his newphew or sister might answer. Okay, I was wrong to believe anything about him, but stop, hang up."

"Hello? What's that you say? Pete's orthopedic what? Shop? Hold on. You in need of a new truss?"

"No."

"Thank you Pete. Oh—Hank. Anyway, thanks, but not today."

"Still, why can't the burglar be the same person who grabbed Donna off the street?"

"Because crminals have done the most bizarre flagrant things stupid and otherwise imaginable, but not that."

"What's that supposed to mean? Goddamn, I'm tired of this runaround from you and everybody else here. Do you know your Sergeant Lux lost the diaries and letters you took from me and doesn't know where they can be?"

"He did? How'd he do that? He might not be the most qualified guy going but he is good at guarding his own fort. They'll turn up."

"No they won't. I'll never hear about them again except, after repeated inquiries from me to the police, to confirm they're lost."

"You can't say that for sure."

"Why not? What've you or any officer given me to make me think differently?"

"All right, maybe this then and you'll go away."

"Why should I go away? Shit, this person I love is lost, maybe killed, and I'm—"

"You don't know that for sure either. And you should go away because we've work every day beyond even how high our arms can reach. It's not that you annoy us. Not that we don't believe you either. But we do have to go on some kind of statistics when we have such a heavy caseload. Insurance companies have actuarial tables, we have this. And in a hundred years of police science and brutality and computers and plain old legwork, we have no record ever where a kidnapper returned to the residence of the person he kidnapped just to make off with costume jewelry and cheap animal skins and radio or whatever junk they had then before stereos and tv's. They've returned to recover more precious stuff or indictable evidence they might have had to stash away there because they were on the run the first time or even for the person who they were originally paid to abduct but who got away. But never for anything so small that they'd chance getting caught and thrown away for life for just to sell on the street for one-tenth its retail worth."

"Maybe they thought she had more than a tv and old coat."

"Why? She couldn't have told them you did because neither of you do. And building and neighborhood she lived in? Maybe middleclass to so-so. Your apartment if they saw it that first time? I've seen down and out junkies who have better furniture and things on the wall and floor. Way she dressed that night? Denims, old sandals with rope soles. Money and jewelry on her? Few dollars probably and that bracelet around her waist which wasn't even gold. Maybe her looks and way she carried herself and talked. But poorer people have that in the worst neighborhoods and with airs up their assholes sometimes and could even look and dress better than most models do, who off-camera are mostly slobs. Her credit cards maybe but almost the poorest people have those in the best stores too. No, a kidnapper or rapist or killer or whatever he is or they are wouldn't have been so dumb to come back and burglarize and he didn't, that's all, they didn't."

"Can you give me advice where to look for her then?"

"Where have you been?" I tell him. "Then you've done it. About as comprehensive as we'd do except without our way with questions and getting answers and authority behind it and cab entries and suspicious reports for those hours and tips we might have received on her which we didn't. No, there's no place else. If she's been kidnapped or any of the other things, then she's been murdered by now and dumped. But what I think is she went off some way and by herself. And that you ought to think about telling her off for all the aches she's caused you the next time you see her, if she lets you, which some day, matter-of-factly, she will."

"Why will she?"

"Guilt. Or her new affair's over if that's it and she's despondent or broke. Or she'll think you've quieted down and are safe to see without you mauling her for what she stuck you through or else to just tell the world about her great fling or joke. And also to see her friends again or whatever, but leave me, will you? I'm way behind today."

I go to room 210. "What is it?" officer there says.

"Nothing." I go.

"Nothing? Okay nothing, you give me nothing, I give you nothing in return and nothing you'll get from me till you give me something but nothing more," as I walk toward the stairs.

At home I phone a couple cab companies who tell me only the police or chief cab dispatcher can have access to the drivers' logs. I go to the post office and buy a dollar's worth of stamps and 5 postcards and 3 aerograms and 2 special delivery stamps and using my left hand when I'm a righty I address a postcard to myself, stick a special delivery stamp on and write "special delivery" and on the other side yesterday's date and "Who: 10 Thou you give, we give back you D. Akers, perfect shape & right away. We know have her—now have her—& know she where denimes blue all, all cloths denimes, all gray shoes made with cloth no lether, & no sox. Wait for contacts from us. Speak to this to Police & your Miss, Sir, we promise, she die." I walk to the main post office and drop the card in the special delivery slot.

I go to all the bars in the neighborhood and those to about 10 blocks outside it and ask the bartender or owner or both if they've seen anyone looking like the photos of Donna I show them and they say no or yes but no one like her in days or weeks or a month and then I ask if they think anyone at the bar or from another place they might know of might have information about this missing person or who might want to make some money helping to get her back or by telling me where she might be. Most of the bartenders and owners say they don't. A few, including the bartender at the Express who spent a night with Donna, say they'll ask around and to have a drink and I buy a wine or beer and leave a good tip and they speak to a woman or man at the bar or nearby table or a couple in back or foursome at a table listening to live music or 6 people playing 3 against 3 on a video sports game or they make a phonecall or someone they speak to makes a call or they take my number and say they'll call or someone else will if they hear anything but if it does turn out well for her or even if I just get a small lead on her from it then I'll come back and lay something nice on them, right? and I say I definitely will, you can count on it, and I'll be tremendously thankful besides, but for now none of the people they speak to or on the phone know anything about where she is or might be or what could have happened to her.

Phone rings. Morning. I say hello and the caller says "Hello? Hello? I can hardly hear you" and I say "Can you hear me now?" when I see the receiver cord's practically chewed through in one coil and she says "Hello? That a voice I hear? Mr. Alimin? This is important in relation to your friend" and I say much louder "Yes I'm here, can you hear me now?" and she says "Mr. Alimin? That you there? Hello?" and I yell "Wait, I'll get it on the extension" and leave the phone off the hook and run to the one near the front door but the caller's hung up by the time I speak into it.

I mix prepared mustard and red pepper sauce and coat the phone with it and phone wires along the wall and put the cat's nose to the cord and he jumps back and I put his nose to it again and slap his behind and say "No, damn you, don't touch it, no." Phone rings. "Hello?"

"You the Art who asked about the Akers lady in the papers?"

"Yes."

"I get both morning papers because I read them top to bottom and afternoon one too. This ad also to be in the afternoon and lady really is missing?"

"Yes."

"I don't know where she is but did want to make certain you weren't using the newspapers to make some sort of fraud."

"I'm not."

Another call. I pick up the receiver, damaged coil, run to the extension and say hello. Caller's gone. I hang up and phone rings. "Hello?"

"While I was having my breakfast this morning I—"

"Excuse me but did you call a few seconds ago or another time a minute before that and nobody answered?"

"No. Before I was having breakfast. That second ago I was dialing. I'm calling because I read your ad in the Tribune today. It was very good and clear and very effective and I also got from it that you are a very sensitive and intelligent man and I only wish I could help you even a little with it. In the way it was written—did you write it?"

"Yes."

"Well I felt very deeply your personal loss for this woman and am very sorry for you and only hope you come together with her soon and that my telephone call doesn't hurt you in any way. I know you must be very busy with many calls pouring in and things to do and that you want to keep your line open for the ad, so I apologize for occupying your time like this and will get off now though did want you to know how you made one person feel."

Call: "You looking—put the ad in the Journal?"

"Yes."

"How much you willing to pay?"

"What information you have?"

"Depends what you're willing to pay and how fast."

"You have to give me some idea you know something before I agree to pay anything."

"Look, don't go bargain positioning with me or I'll sign off."

"I'm not and I'm sorry, but you have to understand that anyone could say he knows something about her and demand payment."

"That's smart. You'll weed out the phonies and not lose all your money for the real ones who can help. Okay—I know she's gone and you're searching for her and who the bastard is, though I'd never say the word to his face, who knows where to get her. That's all I'll give now."

"What was she wearing or holding or looked like that night—anything, her hair."

"She was holding my dick. Screw you." Hangs up.

Tenant at the door. "Someone phoned me just now and said my address is 16 East, correct? and I said 'You know it is, what about it?' It was my brother. He's been here a hundred times the last 2 years and said 'Do an Art Alimin or Donna Akers live there too?' even when I've spoken of you both in the kindest terms to him a dozen times a year. How she's famous and gorgeous, how you're nice."

"I know. The ad."

"I couldn't believe it. I ran right out when he said he was driving over to find out more about it, and bought the paper. I didn't know."

"I've been telling the building for days."

"Honestly, I must have been out each time or in my back room watching television with the sound loudly on to keep out the barking dogs and planes and no one in the building said. I only saw the super an hour ago and he didn't look as if anything strange had occurred. And the Bluds—"

"They for sure knew. But what is it?—excuse me" when the phone rings.

"Mr. Alimin please."

"Speaking."

"I read your notice. Please don't answer this if you don't want to. But if you and the woman you wrote about don't live together or you're moving out for any reason when the 2 of you have lived together and Miss Akers isn't moving back in, does this mean your apartment will become available soon or even 2 of them and if so when and how many rooms are there and what rent do you pay?"

"We're not moving out."

"Thank you."

"So what's the story behind it all?" Mr. Bedoss says when I get back to the door, "because I'm sure my brother will want to know when he gets here and I'm certainly interested myself."

"Have you seen Donna in the last 5 days or any suspicious looking people around or inside the building lately day or night?"

"5 days? Let me remember. No, maybe not even for 10. A delivery boy did unscrew all the bulbs going downstairs and knocked over the plastic flower pot on the first floor, but that was a month ago and I'm sure he meant no harm. But she disappeared your ad says, last seen at the Coliseum—"

"I don't want to talk about it, excuse me," and shut the door.

"Have it your own way. But you won't get anyone's aid you act like that."

Call: "I know where she is."

"Is this the same man who told me to screw off before?"

"What man from where before? You're talking about someone calling, I never did. Donna Akers, right?'

"It was in the papers."

"What papers that? Newspapers? Legal papers?"

"The public notice columns of the Journal and Tribune today, which is usually next to the weather sections."

"I don't read them, weather or notices. It rains, I carry a coat and hat. Sunny?—I can also see that from my window and leave them home."

"Then did a bartender or barowner or someone else tell you about her?"

"No. And if I tell you who I'll be giving away much of what I have to sell you, right?"

"What do you know then?"

"You lost her Thursday night almost late."

"That was in the notices and what I told the bartenders and owners, but you say you didn't read or speak to anyone about it."

"Actually, I did. A buddy dropped by to tell it to me, so in a way I didn't see it first but from hearsay. What I mean—okay. To give you faith in me, the truth. A rang—a man rang my bell and slipped the Trib under my door and told me not to open it, my door, and lucky for you, because she's upstairs in this house. Not saying it's mine, but a house. This man who rang though, he knows. Though not saying anything else about where or what or who I am even or this bell ringer I think is—I know is. Okay, know is, and a ringer, but that's all I'll tell out of my good graciousness now."

"I'd have to know more."

"Look, don't give me any threatening results. Just tell me what you're willing to sell—to listen to—that you are, to me, and next how much cash you have to pay for her getting back."

"This does sound like the man who called before and hung up."

"And who was holding Donna's dick. Is, she holding his. Now

155

holding both theirs—mine and my friend the ringer. Oh go screw you."

Call: "What're you giving away?"

"What do you mean?"

"My boyfriend he called and said you're giving away something that's real good."

"He misunderstood."

Call: "Just wanted to know you're still there." Hangs up. I leave the receiver off. No mail or mailman on the street or from either corner. I put the receiver back on.

Call: "I'm Kitty Salavers from the Journal, paper you placed the public notice in today?"

Intercom buzz. "Excuse me, but the downstairs bell—can I call you back?"

"I'll hold."

Doorbell. "Be there in a second," I yell. I press the intercom talk button. "Yes?"

"Package here for you."

"Mailman?"

"No. Package here for you."

"You want me to come down to sign for it."

Nothing.

"Still down there? Hello?"

"Mr. Alimin?" someone says from the hall.

"Please hold, Miss Salavers, now it's the door."

"I'm here."

I open the door. Mr. Bedoss and another man. "My brother says I shouldn't have riled you and he's right and I apologize."

"Fine. Excuse me but I'm on the phone and downstairs for a package and both might be related to Donna."

"Shake then?" We do.

"Good, you 2 guys are straight again," the brother says following me downstairs. "Now tell me, Mr. Alimin, for your situation intrigues me. Although I know how busy you are, I do happen to be, and my name's Rolph," and sticks his hand over my shoulder to shake, "a lot more than an amateur student of criminology, and wanted to know—"

"Later please." Envelope on the vestibule floor with my name on it.

"That's the package?"

"It must be what he meant."

"Who?"

"Man on the intercom who told me a package was down here."

"Young? Old?"

"You can't tell. The system's scratchy."

"Accent. That should come through scratches and all."

"None."

"Nothing else here." Opens outside door, looks around. "Couldn't squeeze it through the letterbox slot?"

I open the letterbox. Nothing inside.

"What's in it?" as I tear open the envelope.

"It might be about Donna. Even if it isn't, it could be personal. Please, you're in my way" when I start upstairs.

"Pardon. If it's anything about her, such as a ransom or she's been drugged or abducted or anything at variance with her will, read it to me. I am, in many ways more than a seasoned policeman or forensic psychiatrist... I've read numberless treatises and scientific profiles and attended criminal courts as well as been a participant—wait for me, Mr. Alimin... practically a paid hired guest lecturer representing the layman's point of view at club and church seminars and roundtable panel discussions about these things criminal... any type of felonious mind, potentially homicidal or otherwise, so I'm a lot more than an interested party or brother of a concerned but unknowledgeable neighbor in this regard and can help—I can help."

"If I think it's okay for you to read, I'll let you."

"No, aloud, read it aloud now, when you're least prepared for it. Because if it is important then I want to observe your emotional state and verbal interpretation of it to see what you're most shocked about, which wouldn't come out in a more controlled and informed chat about it and which might reveal covert things about her and the situation that you couldn't get in any other way. And my own relation to it will be no more than that of a lawyer to his client, doctor to patient—as you said in your ad:

sacrosanct. This envelope, to illustrate what you can learn. Simple almost childlike schoolroom taught block printing of your name to make it untraceable, like the cheap ballpoint pen ink that wrote it and envelope from any five and dime."

"All right."

"Nat, wait downstairs."

"It's okay, you'll tell him anyway. Just so long as you both don't tell anyone if I say not to."

"Neither of us is married or politically enslaved. I'll only use this avocationally, though without recognizable names and locations, and I'll see that Nat keeps his mouth shut."

"'Art. Do what I say. I'm in great trouble. Drop 75 dollars in the public trashcan on 18th and Traveena, northeast corner 15 exact minutes from now. Then walk away fast and don't look unnatural and back. If trashcan there removed or filled over the top, drop it in trashcan on 18th and Traveena, northwest corner next and then work around clock clockwise till you find one not filled past top. Put 75 dollars in this envelope, though not single 50 dollar bill plus others but anything smaller. If you tore this one up opening it, put 75 in brown envelope 9 inches by 12 size as this one. If no trashcans on either corners of 18th and Traveena or all filled over the tops, though last looked they're not but are trashcans on each corner and at the most filled little above half to top, leave envelope with money leaning up against lamppost on northeast corner Traveena and 18th but facing it to street side. Or even worse luck if street side is filled up with something else, then sidewalk side face envelope but not beside anyone resting or sitting there like a bum. Standing there waiting for red light to change, okay, if they don't see you leaning envelope up. If you can't, then work around clockwise again to lean envelope up against a lamppost or streetlight pole. If every post and pole filled up with someone like a worker working there or bum, leave it under a mailbox on any these corners, again northeast first then going clockwise, even if someone is standing there watching you, working there or a bum. Don't tell anyone of this since it is not a police matter but only between you and I very private. It is my own ignorant mistake I am very ashamed for and will tell you more of once I see you soon. Don't think anything wicked has come to me because of these complicated filled directions. I wrote them so at length because of the urgency to get me the money in the approximately 12 minutes from now you have and I couldn't afford one more mistake. Donna.'"

"You're reacting like it's the real thing. Her handwriting and signature?"

"All typewritten. I don't have 75. I don't have 20, 21 and change."

"Nat, give me a 5." Rolph gives me Nat's 5 with a 5 of his own. "We expect to get paid back. But for now—and this is my learned advice from past incidents like yours I've read—stick a note in the envelope with the 30—that's what these other people like you did—saying you'll get the rest later and for her to phone and instruct you how. Same drop place will be okay for you. But you don't seem excited. Nat before said you were scared to death over her."

"You believe this note?"

"All right, tell me—that's what I'm here to learn about and help."

"Donna's an excellent speller and here there's a k for the c in the word directions and the i in the tion is gone. Approximately with one p, but that anyone could make. And other missing and erroneous letters, maybe some of them typos but most too logically placed to be anything but mistakes, and no capitals anywhere or in 2 sentences beginning every word. She's a stickler for punctuation and grammar which here almost couldn't be worse."

"You're saying she doesn't write or type or speak or even think in any way like this and didn't live most of her life abroad or wasn't foreign born?"

"Yes."

"Let me see it again. Typing seems skillful enough. Neat, few erasures. Manual machine, most common kind of type. Ribbon's reasonably new and holes where the periods were made can be seen through the other side of the page. So we can assume it wasn't typed by a very slight female or extremely weak effeminate man or person of either sex under 11 or an inexperienced typist or one who is arthritic or paralyzed or temporarily injured on one side. Could be she was in a rush or telling you something with her bad punctuation and spelling."

"Like what?"

"That she isn't all right or that you shouldn't think this letter came from her. But that would mean she was forced to write it while at the same time doesn't want you to drop the money off, which makes no sense. No, this had to be Donna writing earnestly or someone not Donna writing earnestly."

"In either case, why only 75?"

"She might need it to pay off someone fast as holding action or the person who isn't her might know you can't amass more than 75 now and doesn't want to risk it for more than 15 minutes. Or again Donna's telling you something that she doesn't want the person possibly dictating the letter, but who might have given her some autonomy on the amount to ask, to know. Does 75 mean anything special in relation to either of you? As an anniversary? Birthdate? 7 and 5 for the month and day, or as in some foreign countries, that month and day in reverse? Anything occur on May 7th or in 57 or the reverse that gives you any ideas?"

"Though there's no mention of him in the letter, her father was around 75."

"What do you think, Nat?"

"Me? You're the expert."

"But I'm asking what you think. Better 2 minds sometimes even if you don't know what you're talking about half the time."

"Father's 75? Drop off 75? She wants Art to drop off her dead father if he still has him and if she is who he wants her to be? Nah. Leave me out of the exegeses."

"You could be warm. Gematrially the number spells g-e. Combination form for earth, ground and soil. One of the 2 spellings for the letter g. Which is the initial letter for his name Gabe or the slang word grand for a thousand d's. Or symbol for the mineral germanium, which is what? In the ash of lignites and coals, which could be what she's circuitously suggesting you do with her father instead of burying him. Or g-5 or 7E for the work rank or apartment number of anybody you know? No, let's forget cryptographs and numerical connections—too subtle or replete with meanings. It's probably what we first said. They think 75's all you can come up with in 15 minutes or all she needs for now. I'd give it. You only have 30 to lose and this woman to maybe find or help. And if you're contacted for the other 45, Donna might reveal herself more or this not Donna who writes earnestly but not like her might."

"It's my last 20."

"She's not worth 30?"

"She's worth 30 30's, but why couldn't she have given me more proof who she is if she wanted me to believe it was her and not write like she didn't want me to know? I just don't fall for it." In my apartment now. I pick up the receiver. "Hello?"

"Excuse me, Rose. —Mr. Alimin?"

"I'm sorry. Something very urgent came up about Donna."

"What?"

"Can I call you back? Kitty Salavers. I'm writing it down. The Journal. Goodbye."

"May I come along as an observer?" Rolph says. "I'll leave a minute after you, walk out nonchalantly with Nat, shake his hand in front of the building in case anyone's watching, then walk to the corner and hail a cab and ride to 18th and Vapor and walk the next block, while Nat slaps his pockets and remembers he forgot something and goes back upstairs. You will have 9 minutes and 2 or 3 off shouldn't matter. They have to expect that nobody's watch is perfect. And you think they calculated to the minute how long it would take to read and believe the letter and get the money and dressed if perhaps you weren't already dressed and walking or running or cab speed over there and time to find one? 4 to 5 minutes off won't matter either. If it is her, as I'll be walking past the drop spot or stopping to light my pipe, I'll know because of her photographs."

I leave the receiver off, on my way downstairs pick up a 10 by 13 envelope from Nat, stick the 30 in and note saying "30's all i got will get more in hr im not hoaxing you please call" and run to 18th and Traveena, walk the last 20 feet, can's filled, cross the street, drop the envelope in the northwest can and from a half block away look back. People pass. Man stops to spit in the street.

I think I see Rolph lighting his pipe. Car pulls up beside can. Rolph's tying his shoelaces against a fender a few parked cars away and smoking a pipe. Another man sticks his hand in the can and pulls out a newspaper. Woman gets out of the car, drops a bag in the can, takes out the envelope, gets in the car and makes a u-turn and drives away.

At home I put the receiver back and phone rings. "Wasn't Donna. Doesn't mean it wasn't for or about Donna but definitely wasn't her. A much shorter and broader woman with a baby waiting in a special car chair hooked over the front seat. I got the make and color but mud covered both plates. Could be you've been bamboozled but could also be you'll never know. Leaf green Landvan, 3 years old. You really want to find Donna, give it to Miss lady newspaper who I heard you speaking to. We'll keep in touch."

Call: "One last time."

"About what?"

"Dick. Holding it. Now I got her and will kill, rape and mutilate your lady and leave her in front of your place in 2 shopping bags if I don't get money, money—"

Hang up, call Kitty. Asks what the ad's all about. "Desk found it enticing."

"Point was to catch the reader's eye but looks like I overdid it." I tell her about Donna from the first night and Gabe dying on the street and how I was just bilked.

"Sounds good. Can I come over?"

Downstairs. Mail carrier's opening the mailbox with a pass key. On her belt's a spray cylinder of mace. Puts mail in several boxes. Then one for Akers. Drops it on the floor. I reach for it. "Don't touch till I'm done." Department store bill. Drops another bill: gas and lights. Then an envelope address side down.

"Bills. That's all we ever get."

"Yeah? Card for you. Special delivery."

"Thought they delivered it special—by truck."

"Maybe leaves the station where it was sent from special but I don't know about delivering it special anymore from the station it reached." Drops it on floor.

"What could it be anyway?" Sit on steps till she's through. We get nothing else but a fashion magazine. Locks up, leaves my mail on the floor and goes. "Goodbye and thanks," I say. Door shuts. Collect the mail and flip through the magazine as I go upstairs. Donna sitting on a bathroom chair demonstrating on her chin "my simple electrolysis instrument that PERMANENTLY removes ugly hair from all areas of my face and also body hair in the privacy of my boudoir." Donna in a lift and on the slopes and fallen in the snow and toasting toddies at a ski lodge bar and in a bedroom threatening to throw a pillow at a man in a 4 page spread. Envelope contains a reminder from her dentist of her semiannual examination and cleaning this week. Underneath: "I'll get you in caps yet like the rest of your colleagues, as I'm not making anything from your cariesless teeth. But after the exam, if your mouth feels o.k., cocktail? Yours, Bud (Dr. B. D. De-Bour)"

I call him. "I don't care if you swear she's been missing 8 to 80 days. Donna's a wonderful person and a pleasure to work on, but anything other than the date of her dental appointment will have to emanate from her." Hangs up. Phone rings.

"I spoke to Pi, night barman at the Plantshed. I'm looking and think I'm hot onto what you desire. Don't accept anything anyone else says till you hear back from me. Cheers."

I call Bo. "Busy," another detective says, "along with Doug and Ted. One will phone back."

Call: "You get the package?"

"I got an envelope, no package."

"You didn't get a wrapped package?"

"If the envelope's not the package, no."

"You'll get it within the hour and contents will tell all. Follow directions to the letter. Wait. —Forget directions, they'll be none there. Just open package and inside newspaper and wait for my call. You moron," he says away from the receiver as he hangs up.

I call Bo.

"They said we'd call back."

"It's urgent. Got a special delivery card asking 10,000 dollars for Donna. Seems real. Can't be related to the ad I placed in the newspapers today about her for it's dated 2 days ago and just got here special delivery though by regular carrier service. Even if it

did come special delivery and was mailed today after the sender saw the ad or heard about Donna but dated the card for 2 days ago, it gives information only the police and Donna and I know."
"Bring it in."
Downstairs bell. "Miss Salavers?"
"Quicksilver service."
Run downstairs. Package. Sign for it, say to the young man "I left my money upstairs," "I'll wait," "I'm not coming down again," "I'll go up with you," "I don't want you to," "Don't sweat," I watch him till he goes, "What are you staring at, old man?" and start upstairs. Shoebox, newspapers inside, and inside the newspapers, a finger. I drop the box. Finger rolls downstairs. I go after it, picking up the box and stuffing the wrapping paper and newspapers inside, but can't touch the finger. Want to push it into the box with my foot but I've only got on socks. Try. Can't. Trap the finger with the inside of the box lid against the stair riser and drop it in the box and cover it. Someone's knocking on the front door. It didn't look like one of Donna's but I'm not sure. Woman and man. I open it.
"Kitty Salavers for Mr. Alimin. Art? Hi, My photographer Ven. What's in the box?"
"Old letters and forms. About to dump them, then thought differently."
"Any for or from Donna I can use?"
"Whatever the police didn't lose I still have." We go upstairs. She asks lots of questions while Ven clicks pictures of me putting on my shoes, tying the laces, sticking the shoebox in Donna's desk, Donna's desk, unmade bed, dresser with framed photos of her folks, me standing against the bathroom wall with a lifesize water resistant blowup of Donna under a running shower cleaning her underarm with a now outlawed deodorant soap, touched up breast exposed, knee covering her pubic region, me holding the dead phone receiver to my ear, seeing that the oven and stove gas are off, looking for my wallet and keys, finding them, cat trying to get its claws out of the couch.
"Yours or hers?"
"Found it soon after Donna was missing."
"Then she adopted you thinking you were lonely or lost."

"That I don't know."

"Just looking for an angle. Here pussy pussy. Doesn't come when it's told and look what she's doing to your couch. You ought to get a clawing pole."

I remove his claws from the couch and cat runs to her to be rubbed. I give her professional photos of Donna and phone number of her modeling agency and say "If you're finished now I have to go to a police station to see a detective. Something urgent but personal and if he lets me tell you I will."

"What is it?"

"I'd rather he give the okay."

"Because so far we haven't much of a story. Tall beautiful thin model missing—I don't want to be casehardened, but that part of it's fine. Comes from an upstate family with famous ancient names and her one surviving elderly parent searching for her in the city dies of a heart attack on the street and her lover of 3 years is more alarmed about her disappearance than the police, that could be tied in too. Last seen walking out of a lousy moviehouse in a fairly dangerous neighborhood at night because the film was too violent for her tastes? Couldn't ask for a neater lead-in because of the rash of recent editorials and news features about ordinary people and legislators and the clergy being once again sick of that shit in theaters and on tv. So much of this violence in the so-called arts and entertainments just for violence sake and how many specialists suggest it encourages kids and immature adults to commit crimes and kill without remorse, much like the iniquitous comicbooks years ago and so forth. But if the police think she left—not the movie theater but left you. Or even the theater, we'll hypothesize, because she might have actually liked that film but only left to get an hour or 2 lead on you because she saw no other way to completely break off, then what can I write about except for that tired social commentary part and your anxiety over her sudden disappearance without the Journal and I one day being hit by a lawsuit from her if she saw fit, impossible as those are to win because of freedom of the press and the Constitution and so on."

"If the police don't begin looking for her again after what I tell and show them today, I'll let you know first what this new information is. It'll be very newsy, I promise you," and unlock the door.

"Mind if we come along?" Phone rings.

"Excuse me. Hello?"

"Got the package?" man says.

"Yes."

Ven's clicking pictures of the mirror image of me on the phone.

"Good. Wait. —What? —Hold on a minute, Alimin," and hangs up.

"What was that?"

"Something about a package I didn't get."

"But you said yes."

"I could have said it to 'Is your name Art Alimin?' but what I said yes to was 'You didn't get the package yet?' Just as I've said yes to just about everything on the phone today. 'Yes I executed Donna, threw her off the roof. Yes I sicced a pack of wild tomcats on her that chewed her to threads. Yes I'll pay a million, a billion to get her back. Yes I'm her father, her brother, her uncle and erotic partner and astrological adviser and husband and son. Yes thank you' to the more rational and kindly ones, 'that's very good of you to be thinking of us, praying for me and Donna's return.' I've been getting calls like that all day from my ad and through people I've spoken to in my search. Like this one I suppose."

Call: "You put the ad—"

"Yes."

"—in the World?"

"That the afternoon paper?" Receiver between Kitty's and my ear so she can hear.

"Don't act naive. You put the ad in or you didn't?"

"I did. I'm Art Alimin."

"I'm one of Donna's closest chums, though unbeknown to you, and from her I'm informing on the q.t. that she's all right but never coming back, ever. The movie was great, straightforward and illuminating and true as you weren't, so good for you, suffer I say, I detest all you scum of the earth birds who think they can get away with any mayhem with women, incest to death.

To molest and nudge us on crowded subways with your talons and tubes, expose us to your babies and venereal rabies and naked bodies on the streets and byways, with your big blue veins and bloated tops and flat buttocks and skinny legs and bad breath and too much screaming drinking and stinking semen and moth-eaten thinking and reciting oh yes old poetry and ferocious plays when you're drunk like young college punks and—"

"Hang up." I do. "I'd like to come along and speak to the detective and maybe Ven take a few shots."

"Can't stop you."

"Why would you want to?"

"Just an expression. Please come along. We can share a cab. You can pay for it. I've no money and you've an expense account."

We leave, front of the building I say "Forgot something, be right back," run upstairs, open the shoebox. Visible bone is bone to me but skin's lighter and finger thicker than hers. Could've become that way after it was cut off. But her nails are long and carefully groomed, with a transparent lacquer, while this one's short, grimy and chewed, hangnail when she had none or always tended to them privately, fingertip nicotined or carotened when she never smoked and didn't eat more than a few carrots a week for fear of discoloring her hands and feet. If I was convinced it was hers I'd kiss it. I put the shoebox in a shoppingbag and old clothing on top to cover it and go downstairs.

"What's in there?"

"Stand by your building for one last shot," Ven says.

"Clothes of hers I have to give to the detective."

"Why?"

"Let's wait till we see him."

"Now walk towards me," Ven says, "stop, little more, stop, turn one step to your left and raise your hand into an indignant fist and shake it at me. Harder. Harder. Good."

Cab to the police station. Bo asks me into his office, them to wait outside. I open the shoebox and say "I think it's a pinky." He says "It's the next finger over which has no name I know of. We'll check it for prints." Buzzes. Doug comes in, shakes my hand, takes the finger out of the box and holds it to the light.

"I'd say male, race goes without saying, about 55, hard worker first 45, probably hauling garbage or the docks," carries it out of the room in his handkerchief.

Bo reads the postcard, says "Write something for me."

"Why?"

"Don't, but you don't, I'm not supposed to presuppose you wrote it?"

"What should I write?"

"Write 'What should I write?' for all I care, with or without the 'for all I care' or question mark, or write anything in our language. Though what you really should write is 'Detective Mallen and friends should boot my ass down the stairs if this card's written by me, though they won't but just might book me.' But that's too long, I'm tied up to here with no time, and if you don't write anything, that's your right—'I've my rights' write, just to keep it short. Or if it's a lawyer you want or think you should have, write 'I want a lawyer before I write one word down.'"

I write "I'm writing on behalf of Donna Akers by order of Detective Mallen and signing it Art Alimin."

Looks at it and the card. "Card's you with the hand you don't normally use and if you want me to prove it, write the same words lefty."

I give back his pen.

"Finger from you too?"

"Quicksilver messenger service. Call them to confirm it."

"Would love to but have to drop by. I'm sure it was a small boy they've never seen before who brought it in with an instruction slip they've since lost and 5 dollars, though neither from you." Phone. "Yuh? —Thanks. Tell Ted to get the car ready." Hangs up. "Doug says prints weren't hers. We'll try finding who by running them through. Now go home. If my superior tells me your little infringement can't be forgiven, I know where you are. But to me she's still missing on her own volition and under no conditions do I foresee any change."

I tell him about some of the calls I got.

"What do you expect? Try skywriting next time."

"At least tap my phone for the ones who are trying to milk me."

"And waste a day getting a judge's order for the tap and another 2 tuning in and 5 in court losing the case if you're not lying to me again and we actually hear and find them? Even if we ended up sending them away, that's 20,000 dollars a year per prisoner it'll cost the already strapped state for your mistake in placing those ads. Mean it. Go home. Leave us alone. Take your phone off the cradle for 3 days and no more ads and bar trips about it or tips to reporters hardup for stories and if I can also shake off the one out there and no other reporter picks it up, you won't get another strange or extortive call."

I leave the office, tell Kitty about the card I wrote and finger sent me and Bo's reaction to it all including shaking her off. She says "Damn, what's wrong with the reader's right to know, and the paper's duty to help, and it was worth a story and now even more so with that finger till you began manipulating the facts. Now the paper will demand I document every one of your allegations which could take days. I'm telling the editor there's nothing much there."

Home. Calls: "I'll speak quickly, meticulously and for the last time finally...." "I saw your notice about wanting a young healthy man of fair complexion and narrow physique to share the driving and gas with you across country...." "Now that Brace gave you the good news about your girl on the phone and everything's hunkydewy again, I suspect you'll pop by the Plantshed I bartend with a generous dividend...." "To start off with, a comparable experience—it was more like a double voluptuary's indulgence really—happened to me—for you see—do you have a few minutes to spare?—I was the person, sensualizing with someone brandnew at the time—somebody I should say and make sure you know I split that somebody in 2—who the ad placer placed the ad about and my first and foremost lover was you. No, that didn't turn out right, though his ad did, so let me start off with again...."

Cat's shat on the floor, ripped Donna's old patchwork quilt off the wall and torn it apart. I grab and spank him, hold him under his front underarms and shake him in the air and yell "Enough, you're getting the hell out of here" and bring him to the roof with a week of food and water and lock the roof door. Hour later cat's on the bedroom air conditioner outside scratching the window. Don't know how he could've gotten there. I open the other bedroom window. Mountaineer's rope hangs from the roof between the 2 windows, ending at the ledge. I still don't see the cat climbing down it. Must've jumped from the roof to the fifth floor air conditioner and from there to mine. Not impossible but doesn't seem any cat would chance it. I hold out a chair with a full back to the cat and he gets on it and I bring the chair inside. For the time being I'll let him stay. I go to the roof, cut the rope, go downstairs with it, take the phone receiver off, shut the bedroom door on the cat and go to bed.

Next morning I'm hungry, have little money, few dollars in my savings account and that's it. She comes back I'm sure I'll be able to explain to her I only did this to gain the means to help her: get a withdrawal slip from her bank, at home copy her signature to it from her last year's income tax return, make it out to me and bring the slip to the bank with her passbook. Bankguards on either side give me the eyeover, teller the money and says "Have a comfortable day."

Box full of mail when I get back. "There are electrical magnetical, and reincarnational forces in our universe that can be called and counted upon, but unfortunately only through me...." "For $5 and 40¢ mailing cost (or mailing cost equivalent in stamps) and a self-addressed envelope (or self-addressed stamped envelope ((40¢ worth of course))), I will send you the typical citizen's guide to being victimized in this city and what rights you have to receive Federal, State and/or/or all three, City compensation and other assistance (housing, kennel, medical, etc.) for these unlawful and vile acts against your family, body, mind, domicile, car, pets and other properties and persons that are legally or biologically and in some instances, emotionally yours...." "What movie _you_ trying to promote thi$ Time _you_ Moneygrubbing Kapitafacit $hitrichpig?" "I have no quartz ball, Mr. Alimin ... that went out with the tinker and milkman, and I hope you don't mind my assuming the familiar with you this soon . . . but I do have, for ten minutes at noon and at midnight each day, an acute futuristic gaze besides a sharp aural perception within a six-thousand-mile radius of Randerbam Lane where I reside. . ." "Artie, it's an old friend of yours, we haven't seen each other for years—I was quiet then and want to remain anonymous now, thus by depositing this card in a postbox several towns over from mine. But my family and friends and I fervently hope everything works out and comes true with you and what is obviously the person you care a great deal for re this ad. If there is anything I can do, which is ridiculous since I'll not be giving you my name and address, but goodluck!"

Under my door's a newspaper article someone's cut out. Journal, page 6. It's about a young mother and her 2 infants who were murdered in their beds last night. The incident is tragic and gruesome but since it only vaguely relates to my own situation if at all, such as happening about 20 blocks from here and where the police have no idea who the killer is, I don't know why anyone gave me the article.

I go inside and put my things on the table and see it's page 5 the person wanted me to read. "If you haven't seen this" is written on top. Byline's K. Leigh-Salavers. Photo of Donna modeling either a blazer, hair product or dentifrice. Small headline: Beautiful Model Missing? Story: Donna Akers, a 31 year old fashion model who is used to earning up to $1000 an hour posing, is missing, but the police will not look for her because she is over 18 and federal investigators cannot help because there is no evidence of kidnapping—an "authentic" ransom note, for example. Donna, who lives at 16 East 12th Street and has been in scores of tv commercials and on the covers of most of the better known fashion magazines, was last seen standing in front of the Coliseum movie theater Friday night by her boyfriend of four years, Arthur A. Alimin. Mr. Alimin then went into the theater, he said, "thinking that Donna was safe and going straight home." According to Mr. Alimin, 43 and of the same East 12th Street address, "Donna was positively not the type to take off and drop her life without a single look back. Even if she did leave like that, she would have phoned—she'd know it would worry me too much." Most of Donna's friends and co-workers agreed that Donna was not the kind of person to leave the city or hide out in it without telling anyone. One top fashion model, who asked not to be identified "in case there is some evil intent and even demontry [sic] behind it and its being directed primarily at fashion models," said that "Even when Donna was leaving a party, she would say or wave goodbye to everyone as if she wanted to make sure we knew later that the reason she was no longer there was because she had gone home." Dorothy S. Bodity, a former top-salaried fashion model and president of the modeling agency Donna works for, said, "Donna probably decided she had enough of being a commodity and human workhorse and simply took off. She shouldn't be hard to find if anyone is truly searching for her. She has the beauty, movement, figure and height of the top fashion models, though she never was one, and she doesn't look like anyone else in the world, which is why she didn't do as well in her career as some women with even less beauty and talent. But you first must understand this profession before you try to understand women like Donna," Mrs. Bodity went on. "Modeling is very grueling, not glamorous, and has a higher rate of potential suicides, alcoholics, drug addicts and mentally ill people in it than any other field but medicine, poetry and professional soldiering. Especially when you have only two to three years left modeling, and with no acting career or active children or starting your own agency or solid homelife to look forward to, all of which I had." But Donna's agent, Beverly Windograde, in a telephone interview from out-of-town, said, "Maybe none of us knew Donna as well as we felt we did. To me, she was invariably joyous and content with her life and the brightest non-academia person I knew. And though I disagree with Dot (Mrs. Bodity) about the casualty rate among fashion models, one thing I know, as does everyone who was as close to Donna as I, is that Mr. Alimin has been excessive in his beliefs that something horrid happened to her and extreme if not intemperate in his endeavors to find her." So insistent is Mr. Alimin that Donna met foulplay, that he sent a ransom note to himself on a postcard and possibly even had a human finger delivered to his address in the hope that the police would think the finger belonged to Donna and that she was in grave danger and would resume their search for her. The finger, Police Detective Bo H. Mallen said, turned out to belong to a small-time rackets figure, whose name he couldn't disclose pending further investigation. Det. Mallen said that either Mr. Alimin had the finger sent to himself or the finger was sent to Mr. Alimin in the hope that he would think it was Donna's and would then pay ransom to the sender to get her back alive. The police believe the second theory is more likely to prove correct. Det. Mallen added that in the last few weeks, owing to the success and publicity given a fatal kidnapping in the city a month ago (see related article on page 23, and editorial on the Views and CounterViews page), there has been an "epidemic" of body parts and ransom notes sent to the families and business corporations the supposed kidnapped people lived with or worked at. Most of these notes proved to be false and some of the body parts weren't even human. Det. Mallen said that charges would probably be brought against Mr. Alimin by the end of the week for not only sending a ransom note to himself through the mail, but bringing it to the attention of the police as if the note were real.

Article also gives reasons why the police won't look for Donna and mentions Gabe coming to the city and dying of a coronary the same night in a midtown massage parlor, which he visited "thinking his pretty child might be up there for some reason, I guess," a parlor employee is quoted as saying, "though we never seen her or anything look like, not that we don't get as pretty girls." I'm described as a husky soft-spoken mild-mannered 6-3 balding advertising copywriter for a publishing company when I told Kitty I cooked for a natural foods restaurant in the advertising district of the city, though I wouldn't give the restaurant's name and address because I didn't want to scare off its customers because of me, when I've actually worked for the past year in the back of a bookstore in the art gallery area repairing and building harpsichords and other early keyboard instruments.

"Donna loved her apartment and the money and notoriety her modeling brought her and we were more compatible as a couple than any we knew, so I don't see why she would have left me," which I don't remember saying.

"I'm definitely penitent about sending the ransom note to

myself and have promised, for whatever that's worth, for the law has to run its course, never to do anything like that again. I must have been crazy at the time. And I mean literally crazy, *really* psycho, so upset was I over Donna vanishing just like that," and he snapped his fingers, "without a single explanation to me *why,*" another statement I don't remember making or with my fingers doing. It also says I now carry a blue loose-leaf binder under my arm everywhere I go. "In it he has written down exactly, pages of telephone numbers, addresses, names, referrals, leads and dead ends since he first reported Donna missing to the police," when all I have is a memobook which was in my back pocket but I think I lost.

Article ends: Mr. Alimin said he was numb but determined to learn what happened to Donna. "Hell, what else can I do, and nobody else will help me. And I love and care for her and will not stop looking till I'm positive beyond all reasonable doubt that she left because she wanted to, or is not being held against her will or because she isn't in her normal frame of mind, or is dead, God forbid," none of which I remember saying but do feel.

I call Kitty and say "You got most of it wrong and I want your paper to retract some of it in print."

"I got it all right, don't tell me. Everything you said I wrote down and have the notes to prove it. Quotes and incidents not from you I have a minimum of 2 people to swear they're true, besides my photographer Ven, who will say that trees are made out of green cream cheese if I want him to. Anything new? Police slap that warrant on you yet?"

"No."

"Phone me when they do, or from where they book you, or I'll call you later tonight."

Answer more calls, read the rest of the letters and am about to call Mrs. Bodity about an interesting insinuation someone pseudonymously sent me involving Donna and Beverly which I don't believe when the doorbell rings. "Mr. Alimin, it's important about Donna." I open the door. Very bright lights, commotion in the hall, camera wheeled into my apartment, man standing to the side of the long lens holding a microphone it seems, people behind the camera rolling and carrying other equipment, neighbors from the building and street mixed in among the camera team and talking about it all and me and the heat these lights breed and then I can't see anything more because of the lights and I'm walking backwards as the camera moves towards me while I'm also trying to look behind me most of the time so I won't fall. Cat scatters. "Mr. Alimin, Spud Lachmar" of whatever call letters he gives and a hand shoots out of the light and shakes mine and he wants to—but there's too much noise to hear him—"Will everyone but the reporter either shut up or leave," a woman shouts and it's quiet—he hopes I don't mind them invading the apartment and wants me to tell him the latest on what I think happened to Donna so suddenly on the spur like that for me to think she didn't walk out on me but was kidnapped—"What is your story in other words?" Camera still moving down the hall towards me as he talks. I move back and say "Is it possible, Mr. Lachmar—can you stop that thing shooting and moving for a second—there's more room in the other hallway—the building's, or on the sidewalk, and the apartment's a mess—watch out for that litho on the wall—"

"No really, it's okay, we'll edit out everything you don't like of what you say. And we'll be very careful—be extra careful, fellas—but we'd like to see the place where Miss Akers lived—Donna—and can you also show us what you think are her best modeling photographs while we speak—this is where she lived with you though, correct?"

"Yes."

"That her cat? Dom, get the cat—under the chair, now under the table there," camera swiveling to the kitchen where the cat was but isn't anymore, then back to me. "Donna have any other pets around? She like pets?"

"She might've once—as a girl—dogs and gerbils I believe. But in the city—we both think it's criminal for everyone and the pets—though not if you have to protect yourself I guess—and I don't have any more large enough photos of her except for one in the bathroom—but that one, besides the place, or else I don't know what television's allowed to show anymore, would be indiscreet." There are about 10 of them, holding sound, light, tv or videotape equipment and wires and clipboards, some with earphones on, all moving down the hall towards me till they force me to the end wall and into the bedroom and half of them come in after me.

"One thing, because it's so unusual and unique, which I want to question you on before we get into anything else, is why you sent that ransom note to yourself saying Donna was kidnapped?"

"As the newspaper article said—it was foolish of me and I'm sorry."

"Cut. Kill the lights. Forget what the Journal said, Art. Answer me as if there never was a newspaper, okay? Okay. Lights." Lights go on. Woman on the other side of the lens from Spud points to him. "Why'd you send the ransom note to yourself, Mr. Alimin?"

"It was dumb of me I know."

"Why'd you send it though?"

"Why I sent it? The police said they wouldn't look for her without a ransom note or some overriding reason to believe she was missing, like a ransom note but of course from anyone but me. So I took it upon myself—on myself took it—decided, I did, one for them, devised one I mean so they'd look—listen, I'm mixed up, can't we begin again?"

"Cut. Kill the lights. Steady yourself, Art, Okay? Calm?"

"Calm."

"I know you're in an emotional upheaval of sorts and it's hot as anything in here from our lights, but just say it was foolish of you and you did it to—did it so the police would search for Donna, because without evidence of proof that she was—now you got me all mixed up. But you know. That reason to believe. And short declarative sentences are easiest. Okay? Okay. Lights." Lights. Woman points to him. "Why did you send the note to yourself, Art—that ransom note I mean."

"Why? The police wouldn't look for Donna without a palpable sign that she was missing. Anything like a ransom note. Also the federal investigators because they had to have kidnapping in their heads. Or rather because there was no evidence or proof that she was kidnapped or had met foulplay. Or at least that's what the—anyway, because I knew something was wrong. Felt it and felt she was in great danger and I still do, I do—no, wait a minute," I feel tears coming, "cut it please," breakdown and cry and lower my head and wave my hands for them to kill the sound, picture and lights, "I can't continue ... excuse me ... I'm sorry," but the lights stay on. "Please—"

"I know how you feel, Art. I'm sorry also. But can you answer only one or 2 more questions? You don't want to, that's perfectly all right. But it is important you do so as it might, if she is being held or isn't but is watching this, reach them or her, and maybe that way one of them will get back to you or us." I nod. "Great. Okay. Has a police warrant, because of your fake ransom note to yourself, been issued to you yet for your arrest?"

"No."

"Do you think one should?"

"If that's what the police decide, then of course I'd go along with it. But that's a silly question and a dumb answer. I'd have to."

"It might seem silly to you and maybe it is, or only to you. But if you were arrested and put in jail, you'd have to curtail your search for her, correct?"

"Yes."

"Now also tell me, why do you think Donna met some form of foulplay and didn't instead go off on a sudden vacation or weeklong backpack tour of the woods or anything like that?"

"I don't want to go into it again."

"You haven't gone into it yet. You haven't actually told us anything about it yet. Let me put it this way, Art: Donna is a beautiful lovely creature with an annual income in perhaps the top 10 percent bracket. And being a fashion model—well they're not known for their intellects but for their bodies and looks, no disrespect intended, as I know that most models work as hard as blacksmiths did and often for 14 hours a day. But since she does make her living that way and doesn't specialize as some models do in only modeling earlobes or toenails or some other part, she has to concentrate on keeping her complete physical appearance in top condition like a decathlon contestant, correct?"

"So?"

"So isn't it possible she decided to hop a plane to a winter playland on the other cup of the globe because the heat and humidity of the city were clogging her pores or drying out her skin and hair? Or maybe because she felt flighty as models are notorious for and wanted to take a dip a thousand miles away somewhere or that backpack trip or anyplace different but away from you. I mean, the world is one big marketplace for models as for almost none of us—and more accessible too, because of the income they earn and international people they meet—so she could ply her wares anywhere she chose to and had the money and contacts to go anywhere too, now is that correct?"

"Yes and no. The chic scene she gave up. And unless she had a second banking and checking account I don't know about, she left all her money behind."

"Then maybe she does have another banking account and in a different name."

"She also would've called me if she left. I said that in the newspaper article and I'm telling you that now. She said she was heading straight home from that moviehouse Thursday night and she wasn't there when I got there and she'd know it'd hurt me too much not to know how she was or where and so that's why I insist that something very bad happened to her."

"You're sure of that."

"I'm sure."

"Neither the police or federal investigators or district attorney and state attorney general's office we spoke to are sure by any means, but you are."

"Yes I am."

"So you're sure she is now in serious straits, like in an amnesiac state or kidnapped or dead."

"That's what I've said and say and said."

"What kind of woman was Donna? Is this your bedroom?"

"Ours."

"And that's your bed. Both yours. Her photos over there. Can the camera pick them up? No, too small I suppose," when the woman on the other side of the lens motions no. "Her parents' photos on the dresser I presume or yours?"

"Hers."

"Which leads me to," and he steps beside me for the first time and holds the mike right up to my mouth, "were you in any way instrumental in the death of Donna's father Gabe?"

"No I wasn't. That's ridiculous and mean."

"She disappeared mysteriously and he seems to have died mysteriously too."

"He died of a natural heart attack on the street. I happened to be there when he died because he'd called me a short while before to say he wasn't feeling well. I don't want to answer any more questions. Please go."

"You're not trying to hide anything from us?"

"No. Get out of here. Leave."

"We've spoken to employees in the massage parlor where it's alleged that Mr. Akers, Donna's father, died 2 nights ago and they said he died in a bedroom there and they said this not only to us but other news media."

"They're lying. You're all wrong. He died on the street. Get the fuck out of here."

"That can be deleted, so don't think you can force us to withdraw by using expletives. But please calm down. I'm sorry we got you excited. The intense lights and heat can often do that. I'd switch them off but we're near the end of our interview anyway. We're sorry, okay? I know how you feel. It won't happen again. Roxanne—tell him."

The woman who pointed before says "It won't happen again, Mr. Alimin. We're all sorry. And I think the interview will be very productive for you and finished in less than a minute."

"Get it over with then."

"Then you're feeling much better now, Mr. Alimin?" Spud says.

"No but go on."

"Good. Okay. Let me resume with these people in the massage parlor who say you came there because they phoned you because Mr. Akers had fainted and couldn't be revived. And that he died during the time they left you in the bedroom with him alone, or he at least was alive when they left you with him and dead when you came out of the room 10 minutes later, and that you then carried him to the street to save, they claim you said, the older man's family name and his personal reputation and face."

"You're going to be stupid enough to fall for what people who work in massage parlors say, well go ahead."

"Mr. Akers was traced back to that massage parlor through

legitimate reportorial investigative work from a flyer from that parlor the police found on his clothing."

"All you have to do is walk in that area for 5 minutes looking for a pack of chewing gum to buy and a dozen flyer guys will pin one of those slips on you."

"But why would they admit it to the reporter? They're not looking for that sort of publicity but trying to shun it."

"Go in again and ask them why. Barge in like you did here."

"That's not answering my question, Mr. Alimin. For one thing, we knocked and asked and you gave permission. Another is that it could be that the massage parlor knew that the best way to avoid further incriminations and getting even deeper into a possible scandal was not to get entangled in suppressing or deliberately confusing the truth but just to say straight out what happened."

"None of what you or they said is the truth, that's answering your question. I've never been to that place and I doubt Gabe even knew it was there or what it was. It did happen to be right near one where he died—I've lived here long enough to know a massage parlor's a massage parlor when they put signs in the windows advertising it as one. But that can't be too unusual a place to die in front of if you happen to die on the street, since there are similar parlors or whorehouses or bordellos or whatever the hell else you want to call them throughout a large part of the city."

"What about the finger sent to you?"

"Drop it. I don't want any more questions or bullshit excuses as to why you're still interviewing me or how good it'll be for Donna but just want you out of here, now out."

"Did you have a finger delivered to yourself to get the police to somehow think it was Donna's and like the ransom note sent to you by someone who had kidnapped her?"

"I told you." I cover the lens with my hand and start pushing the camera out of the room. Several people behind the camera push it back.

"Then I'll break your goddamn lens."

"Don't. They cost a fortune. We'll leave."

"Maybe we better back off," the woman says. "We got enough."

"I'm sorry, Mr. Alimin. We're all sorry. I know how you must feel. I mean that." Just then a man in a leather motorcycle outfit and crash helmet with the tv station's call letters on it comes in and hands the woman an envelope. She reads the paper inside and gives it to Spud. He reads it and says "Only one more question, Mr. Alimin, and I promise that will be it."

"No more." I go into the closet, look around for something to smash the lens. "Get out, get out," I'm shouting while I look. I grab one of Donna's long stubby platform shoes by the tip and come at the camera with it.

"Ask it now," the woman says. She jumps out, clips the shoe out of my hand and clutches me around the chest.

"Were you in any way involved in the disappearance and possible death of Donna Akers, Mr. Alimin?" he says as I struggle to get out of her grip. "Because we just received a bulletin from our newsroom that a teller in Donna's bank heard about her in a published article today and called the police who are going to issue a warrant for your arrest for allegedly embezzling several hundred dollars of Donna's savings."

I throw her down and slam the lens on the side with my fist. The lens doesn't break but the camera swings to the side from the force of my blow. I try shoving the camera over but several people grab me from behind.

"That's enough, let's cut," Spud says. "Lights." Lights go off. He helps the woman up.

"Thanks a lot, you bastard," she says to me. "You ripped my best pants. Any other day I'd make you pay through your nose for them."

"The station will take care of them," Spud says. "How's your eye, Dom?" he ask the cameraman.

"Hey buddy, I covered mass riots and bloody wars before—you think this is anything?"

I sit on the bed holding my cut hand. They wheel the camera and other equipment out of the apartment and shut the door. Phone rings and I run down the hall and answer it.

"Art, this is Don."

"Yes?"

"Hello—Art? This Art Alimin's place?"

"It's me, Don, I'm here. What is it?"

"Hello? Hello? Damn." Phone receiver cord's been bitten into or clawed but not all the way through.

"Dial again," I yell. "The telephone wire's torn" and he says "Art, hello, what?"

"I said dial again, dial again," and hang up.

Phone rings. "Don?" I say.

"Is this Mr. Alimin's residence from the paper?" a woman says.

"Yes, can you hear me?"

"Hello? Anyone home?"

I hang up and sit on the floor. Cat jumps in my lap. I touch him and he scratches me. "You too, get out," and I push him off and look in the phonebook and grab him under my arm and cab to an animal adoption service and give the cat and 200 dollars to the woman there to find him a good home.

"25 dollars would be more than satisfactory" and I say "That's okay, he's a nice cat and I just want to make sure he's not gassed."

I go home and take the receiver off and drink and sleep and try to sleep some more but the fleas keep biting me. I get dressed and go to the police station and the officer on duty says "What's your hurry, you could've waited till the day."